SULTRY NIGHTS

A STEAMY, SMALL-TOWN ROMANTIC SUSPENSE

SERVICEMEN OF BLOSSOM SPRINGS
BOOK 2

PJ FIALA

To the lovely women of my reader group, PJ Fiala's Road Queens, who help me out with names of characters, places, and businesses, thank you. I appreciate you and adore you.

Characters
Amy Burkhart - Allison Valentine (Hanna's Mom)
Vickie Chaisson - Tisha Barkley (Quinn's ex)
Vickie Chaisson - Travis Murphy (Grace's brother)
Linda K. Downing Carlson - Thomas Downing (Hanna's neighbor)
Stacy Hartley - Lance Valentine (Hanna's Father)
Nancy Hoch - Mae Hoch (Hanna's Grandmother)
Brenda Hojonski - Isaac Annen (Hanna's ex)
Kristi Hombs Kopydlowski - Jalyn Hombs (Hanna's BFF)
Kristi Hombs Kopydlowski - Jailisa Burns (Receptionist at Grant Park's office)
Jodi Krill - Connor Barkley (Tisha's father)
Kim Kurtz - Quinn Kurtz (Book 2 Hero)
Terra Oenning - Hanna Valentine (Book 2 Heroine)
Margaret Mathias Park - Grant Park (Valentine Family Attorney)
Elinda Moody - Erin Moody (Police Officer and heroine in Captured by Love, Detectives of Blossom Springs Book Two)

Julie Price - Margot Price (Book 3 Heroine)

Jo West - Jace Marriott (Book 3 Hero)

Jo West - Trey Fielding (Police officer and hero in Protected by Love, Detectives of Blossom Springs Book Three)

Jo West - Imogen Cunningham (Isaac's victim)

Dana Zamora - Carlene (Isaac's victim)

Debbie Zsidai - Monique (Nurse at the hospital)

Map of
Blossom Springs
Drawn by PJ Fiala

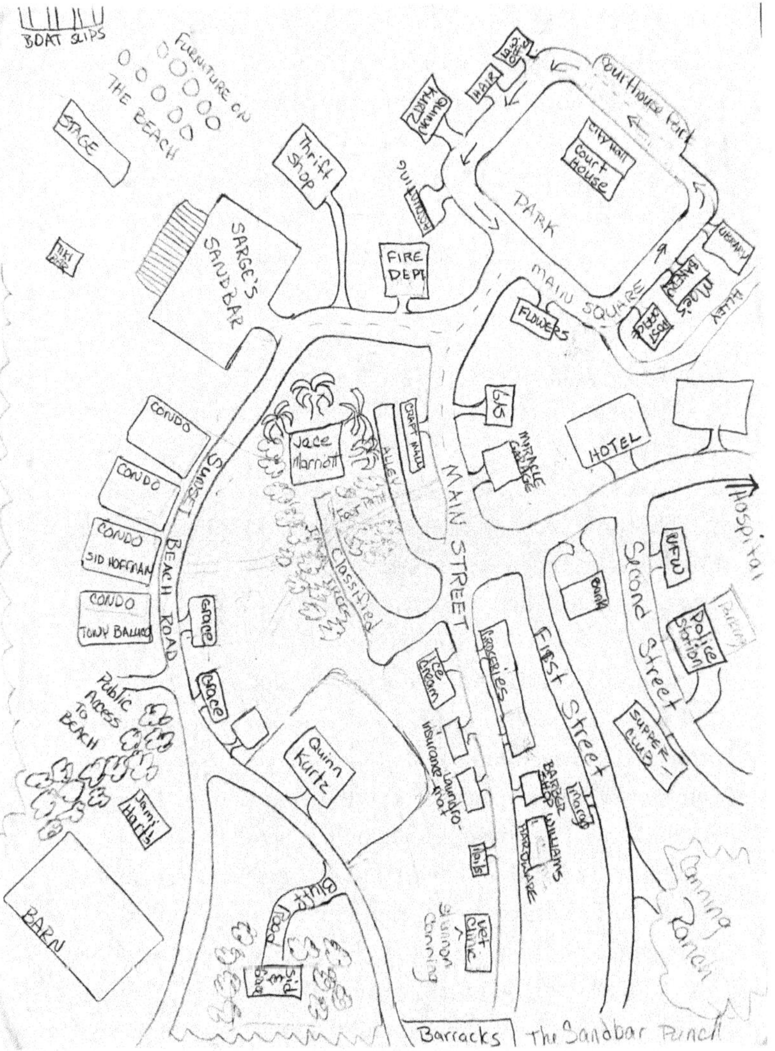

DESCRIPTION

When betrayal comes calling on Hanna Valentine's door again, she must hold on to her dignity and sanity or face the loss of not only everything she owns, but the man she's fallen in love with.

USAT author PJ Fiala, brings you steamy, small-town romantic suspense stories, where outside forces threaten to ruin the peace and tranquility Blossom Springs was built on.

He's finally free of his demons and is ready to start over by helping others.

She's clawing her way back from a situation she never dreamed she'd be in.

They must learn to fight together to rebuild their lives.

Through hard work and financial freedom, Quinn Kurtz has found a way to keep his PTSD at bay. He's vowed to help fellow veterans combat their own demons by hiring them to work for his construction company.

Hanna Valentine was betrayed by a man she trusted and left with nothing. She gathered up her shattered pride and moved on to a cute little bungalow, where she is determined to recapture everything that was taken from her—one wall at a time, and all on her own.

Quinn and Hanna have no idea their pasts are about to collide. The only way to keep from losing everything all over again is to trust each other. But, can a former warrior and a distrustful woman learn to fight their common enemy together, or will her inability to trust force them to go it alone?

USA Today bestselling author PJ Fiala brings you the Servicemen of Blossom Springs series—heroes willing to sacrifice everything in service to their country, and for the men and women they love. A novel with no cliffhanger, no cheating, and a happily-ever-after guaranteed.

1

anna browsed the aisles of the resale store hoping to find the perfect bathroom vanity. It irked her that she had to purchase a fixer-upper, because of circumstances out of her control. But she was making this little place her own. One no one else would be able to take away from her. She worked damned hard; at the bakery by three a.m. every morning and working well into the evening to get the bakery ready for the next day. She mopped herself out of the door each evening only to start all over again, day after day.

She stopped in front of a vanity. It didn't have a top, so she'd have to find one for it. It had a few scratches in it. Running her finger along the scratches, she decided they weren't too deep to worry about. She'd sand it and refinish it, anyway. Leaning forward she picked up the bright yellow tag to see the price. She blew out a breath before turning her head to see another vanity.

Stepping to the second vanity, she noticed it was slightly larger. Bonus. She stooped and bent to see the sides. No scratches. Nice. She ran her fingers along the finish and smiled at the smoothness. Turning the tag, she noticed it was less expensive than the other one, and this one had a pretty faux granite top. Her brows furrowed slightly and a male voice asked, "Can I help you with something?"

She jumped and turned to see an older gentleman wearing one of those bright green shirts with a name badge. Frank. "Oh..." She swallowed. "I was just...no, it's alright."

"Well, that doesn't sound very convincing. Tell me what I can do for you."

She felt her cheeks and her chest warm. "Oh." She took a deep breath. "I was trying to figure out why this vanity is less expensive than that one over there." She pointed. "That one has scratches on it. This one doesn't."

The man nodded and chuckled. "That other one is a name-brand vanity. It has dovetail joints. This one is glued and tacked."

She nodded. "Okay. Well, this one fits my budget better, so I'd like this one, please."

He chuckled. "Aren't you Hanna from Mae's Bakery?"

Her cheeks burned a bit brighter. "Yes. I am." She swallowed to remove the lump that had formed in her throat and took a deep breath to calm her excitedly beating heart.

Frank nodded. "The missus and I love your cinnamon rolls. It's our special treat for certain days."

Hanna smiled. His brows were thick and needed a trim, but his eyes were kind. Fading blue and surrounded by the wrinkles of time.

"Thank you so much. It's my grandmother's recipe. I'm so glad you like them."

Frank chuckled. "I'd eat them every day if my wife, and my doctor, allowed me to."

She grinned. "Doctors and wives always spoil a good thing."

Frank laughed and nodded. "You've got that right. But it doesn't completely stop me from enjoying them. Hang tight for a minute and I'll go get a dolly and bring it up front for you."

"Thank you. "

He limped away and her heart hurt a bit for him. He seemed happy enough and as he moved toward her, pushing a low dolly with old orange shag carpeting wrapped around it, he smiled brightly. He stopped the dolly near the vanity and she stepped forward. "Let me help you."

"No, it's fine. I'm okay. I know I don't look like much these days, but I can handle this."

She wanted to ask if he was sure, but didn't want to offend him. She steadied the dolly as he lifted the vanity and set it on the carpeted area. He smiled brightly, "See? I can still do some things."

"Oh, I don't want you to think I didn't think you could."

He chuckled and waved her off. "I didn't think so. I have an old war wound in my hip. I'm an Army veteran and proud of it. But this old body is feeling the effects of some of the battles I bore."

Hanna's eyes watered slightly. "Thank you for your service, Frank. I appreciate it. My father and brother both served in the Army as well."

"It's my pleasure, little lady. It was my honor to do so."

She wanted to hug him but refrained. He began pushing the dolly with her vanity perched on it, and she followed behind him, chastising herself for feeling sorry for him and herself earlier. There were many folks out there who had it worse than she did.

She sucked in a deep breath and pulled her shoulders back. She found a vanity and her little bungalow was coming along. She still had her bakery, and she was starting a new life. Things could be worse.

Frank parked her vanity near the register. "Do you need to do any more shopping?"

She smiled at his sweet face. "No, this is it for today."

"Okay. Shirley here will ring you up, and I'll help you get this in your car. Or truck. Which is it?" He twisted and looked out of the glass door to the parking area.

"I have my dad's truck outside."

He nodded. "Perfect."

She set her little purse on the tray at the register and pulled out her debit card. Shirley smiled and nodded. She moved the handheld scanner near the price tag and the register beeped.

"That's thirty-five dollars."

Hanna handed her debit card to Shirley, who scanned it into their older cash register. The LED readout came back red and said "declined." Hanna's heart hammered in her chest.

Shirley turned to her, a frown on her face. "I'm sorry, but your card is declined."

The heat rose up her body faster than a raging inferno. She felt the sweat trickle down her back and her fingers shook. She opened her purse and mumbled, "It should work. I'm so sorry, I do have money in the bank." She pulled her wallet from the bottom of her purse and opened it. There were a few dollars inside, but not enough. She pulled them out and counted. A ten-dollar bill, three fives, and seven singles. Thirty-two dollars. She dug to the bottom of her purse and found some quarters. She stacked them four high. One dollar. She began counting out the dimes and nickels in her coin purse when the door opened and a woman sauntered to the register. She stood watching Hanna's shame. Frank shifted on his feet and Shirley sniffed.

Hanna finally stopped counting. Her shoulders fell forward and tears sprang to her eyes. It shouldn't be this hard. Life. She'd done nothing in her life to deserve this.

Her bottom lip quivered, and she sniffed. "I'm sorry to bother you all. I don't have enough. I'm so sorry." She turned to see Frank looking completely uncomfortable. He stuck his hand in his pocket, and she shook her head. "No. Thank you. But no."

The woman who had been standing by watching stepped forward. "Are you trying to buy this vanity?"

Hanna swallowed and took a deep breath. "I was."

The woman smiled. She was pretty. Her nails were perfect and red. Her blonde hair was cut into a short, straight bob with severely straight bangs. Her green eyes were framed with thick, dark lashes. She looked like a wealthy socialite. And completely out of place here.

"Today is your lucky day, then. I have a vanity in the back of my truck that I need to get rid of. I was bringing it here, but I think you should have it. If you want it, that is."

Hanna shook her head. "You don't have to do that for me."

"I don't have to do anything at all. All I want in exchange for that vanity is for you to tell me why you don't have any money."

Hanna stared into her green eyes. They were light and looked almost like they'd glow with the dark lashes around them. Her lips were painted red to match her nails. Her clothing was expensive, and nothing seemed to make sense.

Hanna took another breath. "My ex-husband was a..." She swallowed. "Is a gambler. I think he somehow still has access to my bank account."

"Men. I swear." She sniffed haughtily. "My ex is about to stop paying my alimony. He's filthy rich but is going to stop paying me. I stayed home at his request and raised our two children. Then, he had the nerve to tell me he was done with me. Just like I'm garbage."

Hanna's heartbeat increased. "I'm sorry."

She glanced out of the glass door to see the vanity in the back of a truck. This woman no more fit with a truck than the Queen of England did, but here she was.

The woman stepped forward and held out her hand. "My name is Tisha Barkley. I'm remodeling my home before my disgusting ex-husband stops paying me. It's the least he can do. Plus, my son works in the construction business too, and is helping out. I have a very nice vanity out there, but it doesn't fit my new color scheme. I'd like you to have it."

Hanna swallowed the lump that formed instantly in her throat. She cleared her throat, to completely remove said lump. "Thank you."

Frank grinned. "How about I help you ladies move that vanity?"

Quinn Kurtz opened the door for a woman and her small child at the courthouse. He grinned at the little boy as they passed him. It was warm today. His shirt stuck to his back, and he likely smelled like he'd worked all day in a sewer. But he was going to do this in person this time. For the past five years, he'd been paying alimony while his ex refused to work. They'd argued more than he cared to think about. Their kids were grown, and he wasn't supporting her and her expensive tastes any longer. She could get a job from her rich daddy and leave him the hell alone. He only wished he could see the look on her face next month when she opened her bank account and his latest payment wasn't there. The thought made him smile.

He turned left down a corridor and stopped at the Family Court Office. Twisting the knob, he entered for the last time. The same smells hit him. Old paper and someone's overpowering perfume. His stomach rolled once and he let out a long breath and willed it to settle. He wouldn't be in here long. And, as luck would have it, there was only one other person in line before him.

He waited patiently, listening to the long-drawn-out story from the woman in line in front of him. Her ex this. Her ex that. Men were scum. Blah, blah, blah. It was like listening to his ex all over again.

Finally, the clerk managed to get the woman to move on. He took two steps and laid his checkbook on the counter. "I'm here to make my final alimony payment."

The clerk smiled. "I'll bet you've been looking forward to this day."

"You have no idea." He finished writing his check, signed his name, ripped it from the book, and handed it to the clerk.

She smiled and entered his information into the computer. A printer behind her began whining, and a paper slid out of the bottom.

She reached back and pulled it off the base, looked it over, laid it on the counter, and pushed it toward him. "Congratulations. You've completed the order for alimony. Enjoy."

He glanced over the receipt and nodded to the clerk. "I intend to. Thank you."

He turned and saw two women shooting scathing looks at him. Likely men in this room were not a welcome sight. He didn't care. He'd done nothing to any of these women. And they didn't know what he'd endured during his marriage. It was likely true that any divorced person felt as though they'd been through the wringer. He sure did.

As he exited the courthouse and inhaled the warm fresh air, he sauntered to his truck, feeling lighter than he'd felt in years. It felt good. It felt great. The sun was still high in the sky, though it would be descending soon.

He turned his truck out of the parking lot and toward Sarge's Sandbar. He wanted to celebrate with his friend, Jace. And he'd text their friend Sid, as soon as he got there. They'd celebrate quietly tonight, but next month, right around the time he would be shelling out ninety-five hundred dollars, he'd be hosting a party to celebrate publicly.

Parking in the area alongside the Sandbar, he hopped out of his truck with a new spring in his step. He smiled and nodded to everyone he met as he navigated the sandy beach area in front of the bar. Stepping inside, the lights dimmed, and he waited a beat for his eyes to adjust. He sat on a stool near the end of the bar and waited for Jace to appear.

It didn't take long for Jace to step from the kitchen area, laughing as he usually did. He'd found his own little niche here in Blossom Springs, and he loved his life. The bar business agreed with him, too. He was smart and businesslike, while also being fun and a man people wanted to work for. The wait staff made good money. The bar was growing and full most of the time, and Jace reveled in it.

"Hey, there. Are you all finished?" Jace grinned.

"I'm finished."

"Yes!" Jace raised a hand and they high-fived before Jace turned and pulled his favorite beer from the cooler. "This one's on me. Congratulations!"

"Thank you." Quinn swallowed a fair amount of the cold brew and enjoyed the feeling as it slid down his throat. He pulled his phone out and texted Sid, then picked up his bottle again.

Jace came back to stand in front of him. "Now what?"

"I want to plan a party. Right here. I'm going to see if Hart & the Hurricanes are in town and ask them to come and play for it. I want it to be a celebration."

Jace nodded and grinned. "That sounds like a plan. You having food and drinks?"

"Yes."

"That'll cost you more than the forty-five hundred a month you were paying."

"Worth it."

Jace laughed. "Yeah." He grabbed a notepad from the backbar and a pen and began writing some things down. The door opened and their friend Sid, and his fiancé Grace, sauntered toward him, hand in hand. They were cute together. And they looked happy.

Sid held his arms out and Quinn laughed as he embraced his friend. He leaned forward and hugged Grace, then sat on his stool. "Jace, get my friends a drink on me."

Jace laughed and pulled a couple of drinks from the cooler without asking what they wanted. He had a memory like no one he'd ever known.

Sid and Grace held their drinks in the air toward him. Sid laughed, "Congratulations, Quinn. Here's to a better tomorrow!"

They tapped their glasses, Jace added a drink for himself, and they had their drink. The bar was mostly empty. Everyone usually sat outside on the beach when the weather permitted, which was most of the time. It allowed them some peace and quiet, except for the noises coming from the kitchen: dishes tapping and pans dropping hard on the counter. But it was peaceful despite that. His group of friends were at his side. The only other people in the world who knew most of what he'd been through during this nightmare of a divorce.

Grace smiled sweetly. "What will you do now without having to pay alimony and the never-ending threat of going back to court?"

Quinn thought. He'd lived the past several years waiting for this day. His ex had made it difficult these past many years. The arguing seemed to never end. She could pick a fight with a fence post. He grinned slightly and took another swig of his beer.

"I'm not exactly sure, but I'm happy to find out." What would he spend his brain power on in the quiet of the night? He'd worry about all of that tomorrow.

Hanna watched Frank move the vanity from the trailer behind Tisha's truck. Using the dolly, he moved it to her dad's truck. She helped him load it up, and Frank tied it with rope to make sure it didn't slide out.

"Are you going to be able to get it into your house when you get home?"

She smiled at the kind man. "My neighbor will help me. He's been such a godsend."

Frank nodded and scratched his forehead. "That's good then. I'm glad you have people watching over you." He nodded to Tisha, and she stood a bit taller at his praise.

Frank grabbed the handle of the dolly and nodded. "Okay then, you have a great rest of your day."

She swallowed the lump in her throat. "Thank you, Frank. I appreciate all your help."

His cheeks tinted slightly, but he moved toward the store without another word.

Hanna turned to Tisha. "I can't thank you enough, Tisha. I'm so grateful to you."

"Well, as I said, I'm remodeling my home. My ex agreed to help me by letting my son use his tools and supplies from the shop. Not much help, but my son is handy, and found some things to help me. And to be honest, I'm doing this to piss off that asshole I was married to. It grinds his nerves to know our son is working at my place with his tools and supplies. So, I'm getting the last laugh."

Hanna listened to Tisha speak. Her demeanor was cold, entitled, and haughty. Hanna glanced at the truck. "If you don't mind me asking, is that your truck?"

Tisha scoffed. "Oh, heavens no. Why on earth would you think that?"

"Well, you drove it here."

Tisha took a deep breath. "Right. Well. No, it's my son's truck. He loaded the vanity on the trailer and asked me to bring it here because he was busy. You know, working on my bathroom. So, I figured if I helped him with this, he'd have more time to finish."

Hanna nodded. " Excellent logic." She stepped back. "I better get this vanity home so I can get it inside and work a bit tonight."

Tisha nodded, then held out her hand. "It was nice meeting you, Hanna. I hope you're able to put that vanity to good use."

"Thank you so much. Maybe when I get it all finished, I can invite you over to see what I managed."

Tisha smiled. She hesitated a moment, then said, "I'd really like that." She opened her purse, which hung off her arm, much like the Queen of England carried her purse. It had a brand name on it and Hanna thought once again, this woman was way out of her league. Pulling her phone from a pocket on the inside, Tisha swiped once. "Okay. Give me your number."

Hanna blinked rapidly. Say what now? Just like that? "Oh, ah..." Hanna gave Tisha her number, thinking nothing could go wrong with that. Tisha then tapped away and Hanna felt her phone buzz in her pocket.

Tisha beamed. "Now you have my number, too."

Hanna nodded. "Thank you."

Tisha turned toward her truck and opened the driver's door. "I'll see you soon."

She slid into the driver's seat gracefully and pulled straight through the parking spot and out of the lot. Hanna chuckled and climbed into her dad's truck. Today had a few surprises for her, but the first thing she needed to do was to make sure her ex didn't have access to her bank account, and if he did, figure out how. Then she'd work on her bathroom for a while.

She pulled into her driveway and her neighbor, Thomas, was sitting on his front porch. He was a friend of her father's; they had gone to school together. Thomas and his wife looked after her as if she were their own. His gray hair was always neatly trimmed, his gray beard too. He was easily six feet tall and stayed in shape by biking around town and on the many trails in Florida. He nodded and waved, and she waved back. After she parked her vehicle, she grabbed her crossbody bag from the passenger seat and slipped it over her head.

As she opened her car door, Thomas stood at the ready. "I see you found a vanity."

"I did. It's a good one I think." She held her breath as he examined her purchase.

He nodded and grinned. "That looks like a beauty for sure."

She let her breath out and smiled. "I thought it looked very nice, and the price was right, so no complaints there."

"Gotta love a deal."

"I'll run and get the two-wheeled cart."

She hustled to her house and unlocked the door. She had the two-wheeled cart in the living room just for this purpose. Wheeling it out the door and down the sidewalk, she stopped at the back of the truck as Thomas finished untying the rope Frank had secured her vanity with.

They worked together to unload the vanity, and Thomas wheeled it to her front door. She held the door open as he muscled it through the door, then followed him inside and to the bathroom.

"Do you want it in the bathroom?"

"How about leaving it right here in the hall? I'm finishing up the flooring in the bathroom tonight, then I'll bring this in."

"You got it."

Thomas set the vanity down, leaving it on the dolly. He brushed his hands together. "Let me know if you need help getting it inside."

"I will. Thank you so much, Thomas. You've helped me so much. How about I bring you some fresh cinnamon rolls in the morning?"

He chuckled. "I'll never turn down your cinnamon rolls, Hanna. But please know you don't owe me anything. I'm happy to help you out."

"I appreciate that. Tell June to expect cinnamon rolls in the morning."

He chuckled as he stepped through her door, closing it

tightly behind him. She heard him close the tailgate on the truck and grinned. Just like her dad.

4

Quinn stepped over a pile of garbage in the middle of what used to be a common room area in the closed-down barracks. Staring at the garbage, he noted beer cans, a couple of empty booze bottles, a piece of cloth that looked as though it was a t-shirt, and chip bags. Someone had tried to burn the pile of garbage but didn't do a great job of it. Good thing, it would have burned a hole in the floor, perhaps the entire barracks.

"Dad, did you see this?"

Quinn moved toward Jared and stared at the wall Jared now faced. Graffiti was sprayed on the entire wall. Names of several people, a date that was actually last week. Fuck Politicians. Suzzane hearts Jamal. An upside-down American flag and some little emojis.

Quinn pulled his phone from his pocket and snapped pictures of the graffiti. "I think we need to secure this place to keep those kids from destroying it."

"I found a broken window on the second floor."

"Okay. I think I have some plywood in the back of the

truck. Why don't you grab a sheet and let's board up that window? Then, let's check all three buildings for broken windows."

"I was thinking the same thing. I wasn't sure if you were absolutely going to buy this."

"After seeing it, I want it now more than ever. I'd like to stop them, or at least hinder them from actually burning the place down. Otherwise, I won't have anything to buy." He pointed to the partially burned pile on the floor.

"Yeah. I'll grab the plywood."

He watched Jared exit the building and continued looking at the condition of the barracks. These had been Army barracks for reserve units up until about ten years ago. The Army had moved on to a larger city that offered more in the way of amenities to their reservists and also easier access to food and supplies for the barracks. Since these barracks didn't have a full-fledged kitchen, they needed to bring in food from somewhere, and it was expensive to transport to Blossom Springs. There had been talk for a while about re-inhabiting it a few years after they left, but he'd just gotten word that the Army would rather sell it at a steep discount and not have to continue to pay for repeated repairs, upkeep, and the local taxes on the building. He hoped the decision to sell to him would come swiftly and not drag out for years.

Jared entered the building with a sheet of plywood and proceeded up the stairs to the second floor. Quinn followed behind him.

Once upstairs, Jared set the plywood against the wall and Quinn stepped alongside and lifted the plywood in place as Jared secured the first few screws. They managed it quickly and easily, and as Jared continued to screw the plywood in place, Quinn walked around the rooms.

"What do you think you'll do with this place?" Jared asked.

He continued touring as he spoke. "I think I can make this into housing. We don't have enough here in town, and I think the history alone will make it sought-after."

Jared finished with the plywood and turned toward his dad. "I've almost finished mom's bathroom."

The turn of conversation and the mention of his ex-wife made his body stiffen. Not in a good way. "That's nice," he murmured.

"She wants her kitchen done, too."

Quinn shrugged. "Okay."

Jared scratched his head and let out a deep breath. "I hate being in the middle."

"I haven't put you in the middle. Our divorce is final. I've paid alimony for five years. I'm finished with that. She's had five years to figure out what she would do when I finished my obligation. I haven't asked you a single question about what she has going on over there."

Jared's shoulders dropped. "I know." He pulled his cap off, scratched his head again, and slapped the cap back on his head. "I feel in the middle. She's constantly prying about what you're doing. If you're seeing someone. All that."

Quinn took a deep breath and stepped closer to Jared. He placed his hands on Jared's shoulders and squeezed. "Hey. You don't have to answer any of that. Or you can if you want. I've played this straight up, Jared. I haven't dated anyone since your mom and I divorced. I paid my obligation. I continue to help you and Jenny out. And for the record, I love both of you and I'll always be there for you both. But I made you and Jenny a promise when your mom and I separated. I won't ask you questions about her. I won't pry. Her life is none of my business now, and mine is none of hers. I'm sorry you feel put in the middle. But you're twenty-five years old now. It's time for you to tell her you aren't discussing me with her. If you don't stand up for yourself, she'll continue."

Jared swallowed. He looked into Quinn's eyes. It was like looking in a mirror twenty-five years ago. As Jared matured, Quinn could see it more clearly. Both of them had dark hair and dark eyes. Jared wasn't as tall as he was, but only three or so inches shorter. He was a good kid. A good man. And Quinn was proud of him. But no matter how old you are, your parents are still your parents, and that tends to bring out the insecurity and child inside.

Quinn squeezed Jared's shoulders again. "I love you, Jared. You've got this. Right?"

Jared stared into his eyes for a few beats, then nodded slowly. "Yeah."

"Afterwards, I'll share a couple of beers with you. You'll likely need them."

They both chuckled. His ex could be a handful. And that was putting it lightly. Gawd he was so fucking happy he didn't have to deal with her all that much anymore. The occasional wedding in town or event was it. That was more than enough.

He pulled Jared to him and wrapped him in a hug. "I love you, Jared."

Jared wound his arms around him. "I love you too, Dad."

They stood together for a few moments, then Quinn stepped away. "So, I'm thinking I'll be able to make twelve units out of this place. By merging rooms and bringing the plumbing around, I think they're going to be nice. We'll need a name for them. The Barracks isn't likely going to attract tenants, so we need to come up with something that intimates what it was, but also brings about what it is now."

"Got it. Let me put my thinking cap on."

Quinn nodded and headed toward the door. Outside, he locked the door using the keys the realtor, Margo Price, had given him. He and Jared checked the other buildings, boarded up broken windows, and talked about some of the upgrades they'd make.

After they'd finished, they walked together to the truck. Jared pointed to the ground as they walked. "Looks like whoever is partying here, has a little car. Small tracks all over this area." He pointed to the tracks in the large gravel parking lot.

Quinn nodded. " Great observation."

As they climbed into Quinn's truck, Jared turned to him. "Can we stop at the bakery downtown?"

Quinn's brows bunched together. "You mean Mae's?"

"Yeah. Ms. Valentine's daughter is back in town and now running the bakery, and she makes the best cinnamon rolls I've ever tasted. No lie."

Quinn grinned. "A cinnamon roll sounds great."

"The best cinnamon roll! Seriously, it'll ruin you for any others in the future."

Laughing, Quinn turned them toward town. The barracks were on the edge of town, opposite the town square and his office. They traveled down Main Street, and he honked his horn as he passed Sid's garage. He chuckled when he read the sign: *Miracle Garage. If you see something cool come from here, it's a miracle.* Sid's tongue-in-cheek humor had the town buzzing.

Once they reached the town square, he turned right

and traveled through the first turn in the square and stopped outside of Mae's Bakery.

"I haven't been inside here for years."

Jared shook his head. "You've been missing out."

"I'm trying not to spread out, which is why I haven't been here."

Jared laughed as they exited the truck.

Stepping inside was like walking into heaven. The smell of fresh baked goods filled the room. It was warm inside, but not as warm as it was outside. Cute little tables and chairs were placed near the windows. Two of them had patrons sitting at them enjoying...cinnamon rolls. They were huge.

"Hey there, Jared. How can I help you?"

Quinn turned from staring at the cinnamon rolls the customers were eating, to staring at a gorgeous dark-haired, blue-eyed woman carrying a tray of fresh cinnamon rolls.

"Hi, Hanna." Jared turned toward him and nodded. "This is my dad. Quinn Kurtz. Dad, this is Hanna Valentine. She's taken over the bakery now."

Quinn swallowed to push away the dryness. He nodded. "Hello, Hanna. It's nice to meet you."

She smiled, and it was breathtaking. "It's nice to meet you too."

Her bright blue eyes moved to Jared's. "You're just in time. These came out of the oven about five minutes ago. The frosting is still melting."

"That's my favorite time." Jared stepped toward the counter. "I'll take two, please."

Hanna grinned. "You sure?"

Jared laughed. "Yeah. One for me, one for my dad. He's

never had one of your cinnamon rolls, and I want to be the first to introduce him to nirvana."

Hanna laughed. She had dimples and perfect white teeth, and her dark wavy hair was pulled back into a low ponytail and wrapped with a net. She turned to set the warm cinnamon rolls on the counter, and he could see she wore a pair of jeans that fit her body perfectly. From the front, she was covered in an apron.

Hanna looked into his eyes, and he couldn't have looked away if he tried. "I hope you feel the same way as Jared. He's been my best customer these past few weeks."

Quinn blinked and realized she'd spoken to him. "He has great taste and doesn't boast about much, so I'm sure they'll be as delicious as he's claimed."

He stood woodenly by as Hanna rang up their order, then deftly slid their rolls onto small white plates.

She looked into his eyes as she handed him his order, and all he could do was stare. "Enjoy." She brightly added.

He nodded, took his plate, and followed Jared as if he couldn't think a thought for himself. What kind of dumbass had he just become?

Hanna watched Quinn and Jared saunter over to a table and sit down.

She couldn't help but notice that Quinn's long legs under the table looked out of place. His presence in her little bakery made it feel impossibly small.

He was handsome, and he had a cute little grin. The way he stared at her, well, it kind of reminded her of her high school days when the boys wanted to get to know her a little more. They grinned, their cheeks were pink, and sometimes the tips of their ears were too. They were cute and unassuming, she would say.

Taking a deep breath and hauling her tray of cinnamon rolls to the display case, she quickly unloaded them onto the decorative tray in the case and took her dirty one back to the kitchen.

She rotated her head on her shoulders. She'd been tense. Actually, all night last night and up until just now. It was a relief to feel the tension subside. Maybe it was Jared and his little smile or his dad and his cute grin. Whatever it was, she was grateful for it.

Yesterday after calling the bank, she'd found out that her ex, Isaac, had sweet-talked a clerk into getting him access to her bank account.

That was the problem with him. He could be deadly with his charisma. It's what had nailed her, and that's a fact. Luckily, they didn't have children, though she'd love to have a sweet little one to hold.

But having a child with Isaac would have been horrible. He was a terrible person. Her parents seemed to know it from the start, but she wouldn't listen to them. She'd been so besotted by that ass.

Anyway, after finding out he sweet-talked the clerk, she was worried that anybody else could be taken in by him, too. She asked the bank what their controls were as far as moving forward and that no matter who he sweet-talked or tried to get to; he did not have permission to access her account, or anyone else's for that matter.

The bank assured her they'd taken steps to secure accounts and were doing a full forensic audit of the banks' accounts now that they'd uncovered this breach.

The clerk had been fired, and they were retraining employees at this moment on protocols. That helped ease her mind a little bit, but it didn't help the fact that he had still done it. And she wanted her money back. The bank had replaced the money Isaac had taken this last time. She now wondered if he'd done it before in smaller amounts and she hadn't noticed. She was so busy at the bakery every day, and working on her little house at night, that she didn't have time to check her accounts. Maybe her dad would take that on, too. Oh, she dreaded the conversation they'd have over this.

For the time being though, she needed to make this bakery her cash cow. Her grandmother started the bakery, and her mother ran it for years. And while it hadn't made them millionaires, the bakery had always provided their families with a certain amount of security.

She hadn't intended to come back and run the bakery, but her mom's hands couldn't handle the workload anymore, and she begged Hanna to come back to Blossom Springs to keep the family bakery going. Since she was getting *un*married, the timing was perfect.

Her grandmother, Mae, had named the bakery after herself: Mae's Bakery. And Hanna was determined now, more than ever, to make sure that it was successful.

Luckily, years ago when she had married Isaac, her parents had demanded that everything that was in her name remain in her name. They'd kept things separate, including the bakery bank account. Her father demanded Isaac never have access to that account. She'd been mad at first. Oh, she loved him. He'd never hurt her. And why were they being so cruel?

And now, as she thought back on it, she really owed her parents an apology and a big thank you for keeping at least this part of her security safe from him.

She picked up a tray of cookies that had been cooling and walked them out to the bakery. The second she walked out of the kitchen door, her eyes met Quinn's.

She smiled and felt the heat rise up her chest and her cheeks. And it actually made her feel a little giddy. The last thing she needed to be was giddy.

She transferred her cookies to the more decorative tray in the display case and then wiped the crumbs that had fallen. She couldn't help but glance over at Quinn now and then. And it always seemed when she looked at him, he was looking at her.

Picking up her dirty cookie tray, she moved back to the

kitchen, set the tray on the counter, and leaned forward with her palms on the steel table. Taking a few deep breaths, she told herself to straighten up. It was just a cute little flirtation. And goodness, it felt wonderful.

She didn't need to dwell on that now, good Lord. She was just getting rid of Isaac and hadn't even done that completely, the way he continued to interrupt her life.

The last thing she needed was another man.

Her phone rang. She deftly reached back and pulled her phone from her back pocket.

"Hello, this is Hanna."

The female voice on the other end of the phone sent a chill right through her.

"Hanna Valentine, you owe me twenty-three thousand, five hundred and eighty-two dollars."

Her heart beat so fast she had a hard time catching her breath. "Excuse me?"

The voice came back. "You heard me. You owe me money."

"I don't even know who you are."

"Well, let me tell you who I am. I'm Imogen Cunning-ham. Your husband, Isaac Annen, has stolen money from me."

Hanna's voice was small, her throat was dry. Her heartbeat wouldn't settle. And now she was finding it diffi-cult to breathe. Moving across the kitchen to the wall, she leaned her back against it and dropped her head back to fully support herself.

"I don't know how he stole money from you, but that has nothing to do with me."

Imogen was pissed. Her voice sounded tense and every word that came out of her mouth was clipped. "Your husband, and I use that term loosely because clearly you don't know what he's up to." She took a shaky breath. "He catfished me. He promised he was coming to marry me. He asked for money to start up his new business. He asked for money to travel to come and live with me and said the whole time that you kept taking that money, which is why he had to keep asking. Now I tell you, I want my money back."

Hanna closed her eyes for a moment. This couldn't be happening. My God, what next? This man was unbelievable. Isaac Annen was nothing but a piece of shit. How could she not have seen that all these years? And, how on earth did this woman track her down after she'd gone back to her maiden name after the divorce? She wasn't going to ask that right now.

Her hand shook as she held the phone to her face. She took in a deep breath. It was important to sound strong when she could finally respond.

Fear was the last thing she wanted to impress upon Imogen, but good God, she was afraid.

"Look, Imogen, I'm very sorry if Isaac has duped you. Believe me, he's duped everyone in his life. I've never stolen a thing from Isaac. As a matter of fact, just last night, he stole money out of my bank account. He sweet-talked a clerk into giving him money. My money. So I'm here to tell you now, I don't owe you anything. Isaac and I are divorced. I've never gotten any money from you. He has. You'll need to sue him, not me."

Imogen was quiet for a minute on the phone. Hanna could hear her breathing, which was a miracle because her heart beat so hard it was all she could hear in her own ears.

She felt pity for this woman. Lord Isaac had put her through so much, now he was doing it to another woman.

Geez, would he never cease to amaze her at what he was willing to do to others.

Imogen finally said, "I will find a way to get my money back. But I do believe you are somewhat responsible for that theft. I'm going to find a lawyer that will agree to that, one way or another. Either you or Isaac or both of you are going to give me my money back."

The call ended with a little beep. And not for the hundredth time since she'd been dealing with Isaac, Hanna so wished the old-fashioned phones were still in existence so she could slam the receiver down.

Instead, she was left with tapping her end call and closing out her phone app. She tucked her phone in her pocket just as the bell over the door signaled another customer.

She swallowed, and brushed her fingertips over her forehead to try to smooth the lines she knew had just formed there from her confusion, frustration, anger, and irritation, all the things that Isaac signaled in her.

She inhaled a deep cleansing breath, plastered on a fake smile, and stepped out to the bakery.

Yes, Quinn's eyes were on her. Hers met his. She tried to smile. She knew it looked fake. The way he sat back quickly told her she was not an actress and should certainly keep her day job.

She turned her attention on the older lady standing at the display counter.

"Good afternoon, Miriam. How can I help you?" She faked.

6

Quinn sat at a conference table in Price Realty's office.

Margot Price, a very pretty fifty-some-thing-year-old woman who owned Price Realty, entered with a smile on her face.

"So here we go. Are you ready?" She asked.

Quinn nodded. "Yup, I'm ready. Let's do it."

Margot laid paperwork in front of him. "This is your offer. It's a little more complicated than just a regular offer. You know, the Army has their little idiosyncrasies that they have to have in each offer. But take a look at the price." She pointed her pen at the amount he was offering. "If that's correct, then the next thing we'll move to is the closing information."

She moved her pen down to the date, one month from today.

"Will that be sufficient? Will you have funding by then?"

Quinn shrugged. "I have funding already, so I don't have to worry about that. I'll be paying cash."

Margot's eyebrows shot up in her dark bangs. "Cash? You're paying cash for this?"

He grinned. "I've set money aside after some great business deals. I have money from my grandfather that has been in a trust for years. And yes, I'm paying cash for this."

He grinned, and she laughed. "Well, okay then. That changes the story a bit. You can close whenever you want. If you want to close before one month, I can write that down in the offer."

He shrugged. "It'll take me about four days to get the money gathered up. What the hell? Let's throw it out there as one week. Let's see if they'll bite."

Margot shrugged. "It might take more than a week for them to even get this offer to the person who needs to see it. But hey, what the hell? Let's try it."

She scribbled on the paperwork, changed the date, and they continued to move through the items he wanted in his offer. Basically, there wasn't much to change. There was no title that the Army was willing to give other than there were no liens or encumbrances on the property. They would offer him that. Anything else was as is. They weren't guaranteeing anything inside; the plumbing, the electrical. The condition was the condition. He had to agree he wouldn't be coming back to them for anything else, and he was fine with that.

He knew the building was older. The plumbing and the electrical would all have to be rerouted to make up new units. So that was a moot point.

Once they gutted everything, he'd start all over. It would be worth it. Otherwise, he'd be fixing things all the time. So he may as well start out fresh. And this was going to be a big thing for him. Kurtz Construction was doing well. He was grateful for that. He'd worked hard for years to make his company viable. But this was going to be the thing that he wanted to be known for.

This was the thing that was going to get the attention of people all over the state. And that's what he was banking on. He hoped other businesses would do the same thing. Repurposing old buildings was wonderful for the town.

Margot made the changes and printed off a new copy.

He scribbled his name and the date at the bottom.

She pulled the paperwork toward her, reached across the table, and shook his hand.

"Okay, let me go do my work. I'll be in touch as soon as I hear anything."

He grinned and nodded. "Thanks, Margot. I appreciate it. You're great at this."

She chuckled. "We'll see. You can tell me that after we make this deal come through. In the meantime, you can start gathering your financing. If they come back, it'll probably be a day or two before closing and we're not going to have a lot of time."

He shrugged. "Okay, we'll see when we get it. In the meantime, I'll get everything ready. See you soon."

He left the Price Realty building feeling better than he'd felt in a long time. This was a big step forward.

As he walked outside, the humidity of the day was already at high levels. The sun was high in the sky and he was eager to get back and tell Jared that he'd placed the offer they discussed yesterday. He'd make Jared the sub-general on this. It would be the first time he managed a big project, and he was going to do it right alongside his dad. Quinn was excited about the opportunity to work this closely with Jared and give him a big start in the construction business. After all, he hoped one day the construction company would be Jared's. So no time like the present.

"Let's get this boy trained up right," he said out loud.

Hopping in his truck, he turned toward Sarge's Sandbar. He was excited to tell Jace the good news. Then he'd head to work.

He also wanted to check out how his party planning was shaping up. Parking the truck, he sauntered into the bar, sat at the end, and waited for his friend, who he knew was in the kitchen, directing traffic, getting things ready for the lunch crowd that was coming up in just about an hour, and whatever else he had to deal with back there. Before long, Jace stepped out into the bar.

"Well, hey. I didn't know you were here. Why didn't you say something?"

Quinn shrugged. "I know what it's like to own a business. I was just letting you do your thing back there. I figured you'd show up, eventually."

Jace threw his head back and laughed. "Ah, you know me well, friend. You know me well. So what's going on? You're normally not here during the day."

Quinn rapped his knuckles on the bar a couple times. "I just put an offer in on the old Army barracks."

"No shit! Awesome! What are you going to do with that?"

"I'm going to turn it into apartments. I think I can get twelve units out of each building. When we get inside and plan in earnest, I'll see. Maybe I can condo it out."

Jace nodded. "That would be perfect. Condo it. Then owners can Airbnb it, rent it out, or live in it. We're in need of short-term rentals here in town."

"Yeah, it's a thought. I'm going to think about it. I'd

have to go to the town board for that. So no promises. But anyway, that's on the agenda for me. Now I'm just waiting to hear if they'll accept my offer. So, I figured I'd stop and check in with you about the party. What do you need from me?"

Jace laughed. "We're still on track, and I don't need anything from you. I've got food ordered. I've got everything I need. Staff has been informed about the party. All you need to do is see if Hart & the Hurricanes are in town and if they'll be playing. Because if so, I'm going to need to get a stage set up. Rather than renting one all the time, I've been thinking about building one.

"So I'm thinking I might have enough time, and I know this guy who owns Kurtz Construction Company, and thinking maybe he and his crew might have enough time to build me a nice stage. What do you think, bud? Can you get a new stage built before your party?"

Quinn laughed. "Well, we've got some projects going on right now, but I bet you I can spare a couple guys to get over here and start building a stage. Why don't we walk outside and see where, and how big you want it, and then I can have some guys come over and actually do the estimate for supplies and such? Deal?"

"Yup, that's a deal."

Quinn stood up just as the door opened. Backing into the door was the finest butt he'd seen since... yesterday actually. Cute, adorable, and squeeze-worthy. And then the rest of her appeared.

Hanna was backing in the door carrying a big box of bakery items and when she turned and saw him watching her, she froze.

He hurried toward her. "Hey, let me take those for you."

She blushed, and it was adorable. But when he grabbed the boxes from her, she held kind of tight. "You don't have to, I can do this."

He nodded. "I'm sure you can. Just let me help you. Look, chivalry is not dead. Let me prove it to you."

Her shoulders relaxed a little bit and that beautiful smile he'd seen yesterday greeted him.

"Okay, I'm sorry. I'm just trying not to rely on a lot of people right now and do things myself."

He shook his head. "I don't know why you'd do that when somebody's offering to help you. Let them help."

"Well, anyway, thank you," she said. She turned and stepped out to her van. "I have more things. I'll be right back in."

Quinn turned and saw Jace staring at him, a sly grin on his face, and he rolled his eyes.

"What?"

"Nothing. That was cute. I thought it was cute. You being chivalrous and all."

Quinn shook his head, "Fuck you."

Jace threw his head back and laughed again. "Yep, that's exactly what I thought." He walked over and took the boxes from Quinn.

"Freshly baked bread for my sandwiches at lunch and just in time. The chef in the back was complaining that he hadn't seen the bread yet."

Quinn shrugged. "Well, it's here now and it couldn't be any fresher. Tell him to stop complaining. Your customers are going to be thrilled."

Hanna's butt pushed the door open one more time, and he hurried once again to help her. This time, she only had one box, and it wasn't nearly as large.

She smiled again. "I've got this one. Thank you, though."

She breezed past him while the aroma of freshly baked bread and cinnamon rolls reached his nostrils. He followed her to the kitchen and watched as she set the baked goods on the metal table in the middle of the room. The chef had already pulled the bread from the other boxes and the kitchen staff was quickly putting away things that they didn't need immediately.

Jace walked over and looked at the last box that Hanna brought in and lifted the lid. His eyebrows went up into his hairline.

"Cinnamon rolls? I didn't order cinnamon rolls."

She laughed, "I know, but I'm so grateful for the business you've given me that I'm sharing these with you and your staff. So enjoy and thank you again for all the business you've given me."

Jace nodded. "Now that's the way to do business. Thank you, Hanna Valentine. I certainly appreciate that."

As soon as Hanna said they were for the kitchen staff, everybody in the kitchen within hearing distance descended on the box and there wasn't a roll left within three minutes.

Quinn stepped back and held his hands up in the air. "Wow, let me get out of the way."

Hanna chuckled. "I love seeing everybody so happy with my cinnamon rolls. You don't know what it does for me."

She turned to leave the kitchen, and glanced over her shoulder at Jace. "Same amount tomorrow?"

Jace nodded, "Yep, same amount please, but then heads-up for Saturday. We're going to need double.

There's a fishing tournament in town. I'm expecting a bigger crowd for lunch."

"You got it." Hanna turned to leave and Quinn followed her.

"Your cinnamon rolls are going to rock this town, Hanna."

She turned her head as she walked. "Thank you. I hope so. It's what I'm going to used to make my mark on this town, I guess."

He chuckled. Hadn't he had the same sentiment about the old barracks? "Well, couldn't be a better way to make your mark than that. That's a fact."

He hustled in front of her and opened the door, and she stepped out into the sunlight. The sun shone on her dark hair and he could see little ribbons of auburn streaked through. It was pretty. She was pretty.

In the sunlight, he could see how blue her eyes were. She was stunning.

"So I was wondering if you'd like to have dinner with me."

It came out, and he was almost as surprised as she was.

Her eyes opened wide, and she stared for a minute.

"Well, I didn't expect that."

He chuckled. "Actually, I didn't either. But would you like to have dinner with me?"

"It's not that I'm not interested. It's that—"

He finished for her. "You're not interested?"

"Well, it's just... it's not you."

"Oh," he said, "don't tell me. It's not you, it's me. Oh, don't give me that line. That is old and overused."

She chuckled. "I've just gotten out of an ugly divorce

and I'm still dealing with junk, and I don't know what to say."

Quinn nodded. He swallowed the lump that was quickly forming in his throat. "Say yes. I've just finished paying off alimony and went through a wicked divorce myself. I'm not looking for anything other than some good conversation and to learn a little bit more about Hanna Valentine, cinnamon roll baker extraordinaire. Since you have my son hooked on your cinnamon rolls, the least I could do is get to know his dealer a little bit better."

She laughed, and he enjoyed watching the joy on her face and those dimples. Good Lord, those dimples.

She finished laughing. He saw her swallow before saying, "Okay, dinner."

He grinned. "How about if I pick you up at your place tonight, around seven?"

She ran her hand over the top of her head, pulling stray hairs back into her ponytail. "How about if you meet me at the bakery at seven? I'll likely be working to prepare for tomorrow, anyway."

He nodded. "I can do that. I'll see you at seven, Hanna."

"Yes, see you at seven."

She smiled, hesitated a moment, and then turned and climbed into her SUV.

He watched as she pulled away from the bar and then he heard laughing.

He turned to see his friend, Jace, leaning against the door jamb, holding the door open with his butt, staring at him. "I'll see you, Hanna," he teased.

Quinn shook his head, "Fuck you. Let's go out and look at where you want this stage built."

Jace laughed and strutted across the sand.

Quinn followed. He wasn't going to hear the end of this.

7

Hanna fanned herself with her right hand while gripping the steering wheel with her left. It was sure warm today. She pushed the blue arrow up, on her console to turn the air conditioning up a couple of notches.

Her stomach still fluttered with butterflies as she passed the other businesses in town to get to the bakery. Quinn Kurtz was as handsome as he was charismatic. That stopped those butterflies from flying. Was she nuts? The last thing in the world she needed was another charismatic man in her life. Hadn't Isaac twisted her around enough for the rest of her life? She should look up Quinn's number and call tonight off. This was a bad idea.

Just as she put her SUV in park behind the bakery, her phone rang. She jumped when it did. Her mind had been on other things.

She saw her friend, Jalyn's name on the screen and pushed the button on her steering wheel to answer the call. "Hey, girl. How are you?"

"What's wrong? You sound stressed."

She let her breath out, and it also deflated her shoulders at the same time. "Oh, Jalyn. I'm a mess." Her bottom lip quivered. She had so many things going on right now. She could feel all the tears rushing to the surface even now.

"No! What's wrong?" She took a breath. "Wait. I'll come to the bakery around two o'clock. You can tell me in person."

She sniffed. "Okay." She managed to get out without bursting into tears.

"Okay. Hang tight. I'll be there then."

The phone went dead. Hanna sucked in a few breaths and got herself under control. Blowing out one last breath, she exited her SUV and trudged up the sidewalk to her bakery. One last big breath before entering. She plastered on a fake smile and opened the back door.

"Hey, there. That didn't take long." Her mom smiled brightly at her.

She watched her mom fumble slightly with the spatula as she moved the cookies off a baking pan and slid them onto the tray. Her hands didn't work like they used to. The arthritis had stiffened her knuckles and bent them out of shape. Her stomach dropped at the sight of the struggle, but she swallowed the lump that had formed and continued into the kitchen.

"No, it doesn't take long. Thank you for sitting here and helping out. I sure do appreciate it."

"Oh, honey. Of course. I kind of miss it, you know? So, I'm happy to come for an hour or so while you do deliveries."

"Thanks, Mom."

"Are you okay, honey? You seem down."

"Yeah. I'm fine, Mom. I'm just..." She was what?

Dealing with Isaac's shit again? Some woman wanted thousands of dollars. Her own bank account had been drained. And, she made a date she had no business making with another man who was handsome and charming? She sounded simply pathetic.

"Just what honey?"

Stupid. She was stupid and gullible. "Tired."

"Oh, honey, between fixing up your place and the bakery, you're working far too hard."

There were those tears again. Her nose tickled as the feelings washed over her. Softly she said, "Yeah. I might close early today and take a nap."

"Oh, now that's a great idea. You can go right now if you need to. I can stay a while longer."

"Mom, I don't want you to have to do that."

"It's no problem, honey."

She let her shoulders fall. She stopped her hand from pulling her apron off the hook it hung on near the door. Her mind whirled around all she needed to do. But, a nap couldn't hurt that much, could it?

Deciding to take a break, she nodded. Thanks, Mom. I won't be gone long."

Her mom smiled and waved. She was still a pretty woman. Hanna had gotten her dark hair from her mom. She'd gotten her blue eyes from her father. Her height from her mom. She stopped growing at five foot one. She'd even gone so far as to sit in a tree as a young girl and Jalyn tied heavy rocks to her ankles using an old t-shirt and let them hang hoping her legs would stretch. Jalyn was tall. Five foot eight. But Hanna never did grow another inch. It was frustrating.

She silently stepped outside into the heat of a summer afternoon in Florida. The temperature was close to its high today. Ninety-five was the weatherman's announcement this morning. Stay hydrated, he'd said.

She climbed into her SUV and started it up. There was no time better than the present. She drove down the alley behind her business, and others', turned left onto the square, and a slight left onto Main Street. Staying left at the fork, she drove past the fire station where Jalyn worked. She was Blossom Springs's very first female firefighter, and Hanna was incredibly proud of her best friend. They'd been friends all through school and into their adult lives. Hanna moved away to go to college at her first choice in Colorado to further enhance her knowledge of baking and culinary skills. Jalyn went off to learn how to be a firefighter like her father was before her.

Jalyn was outside, polishing one of the fire trucks. Her friend waved at her and trotted toward her as Hanna lowered the window.

"Hey, what's up? Couldn't wait to see me?"

"They have you out here polishing that damned truck? It's hot as blazes out."

Jalyn laughed. "Need I remind you I fight fires? Nothing's hotter than a building on fire."

Hanna shrugged. "Ya got me there."

Jalyn leaned her elbows on the sill where the window had been. "What's going on with you?"

"Mom's at the bakery and told me to go home and take a nap, but I won't sleep because I've got too much on my mind. I didn't know if you were off today or not."

Jalyn looked at her watch. "I'm off in five minutes. I was going to go home and shower before coming by you, but if you wait here, I'll run in and grab my purse and you can take me home while we talk."

"How did you get here if you need a ride?"

"I walked."

"You're nuts."

"I've been told. Hang tight." Jalyn patted the door and turned.

Hanna watched her tall, thin friend jog into the fire station. Two of the male firefighters were still polishing the fire truck. She waved and smiled, and they waved back.

Jalyn reappeared and jogged toward her car. She hollered goodbye to her co-workers and hopped into Hanna's SUV.

"Okay. All set."

Hanna put her SUV in drive and slowly pulled away from the curb.

Jalyn didn't wait too long. "Tell me what's up."

Hanna told her about the thrift store a couple of days ago and her pathetic bank account. "I called the bank yesterday to find out just what had happened, and after some back-and-forth phone calls most of the day, they came back with the news that Isaac had sweet-talked that new little red-haired clerk into giving him access. Apparently, he told her he was related to the bank president, and it would be okay this one time. He claimed I'd stolen money from him and he just wanted it back."

"That son-of-a-bitch."

"Yeah." Hanna turned into the subdivision Jalyn lived in. "That's not the half of it. Yesterday, a woman called me and told me Isaac had stolen more than twenty-thousand dollars from her and she wanted me to pay her back. Claimed I'm as much to blame as he is."

Jalyn turned in the seat and stared at her. "Are you making shit up?"

"No!" She raised her voice.

"Over the years, that stupid bastard has pulled some bullshit on you. My gawd, how many cars of yours had he gambled away?"

"Three."

"Three fucking cars. That you had to work your ass off to pay for when you didn't even have them anymore. Three! And I believe the last two he forged your name on the title. He should be in jail for that."

She yelled it as if Hanna didn't remember. It had been seared into her mind.

"And then, didn't he try to use your house as collateral on a football bet?"

"Yes."

"Yes. He sure as hell did. But did you leave him?"

Tears escaped her eyes and slid down her cheeks as her shame was tossed at her again. "No."

"No." Jalyn turned toward the windshield and crossed her arms over her chest as if she had been the one cheated and stolen from.

Jalyn sat quietly even though Hanna had pulled into her driveway. After a few moments, she turned her head toward Hanna. "I'm sorry."

Hanna swiped at the tears of shame that once again stained her cheeks. "I know you are."

"I love you, and I get so pissed when this fucker hurts you. We thought you were finished with him."

"I know." She pulled a tissue from the box in the center console and swiped under her eyes.

"What did he do to steal the money?"

He catfished her. Said he was going to marry her. Said he was starting a business. Said I was stealing her money from him and that's why he kept asking for more. So he could get away from me."

"Mother. Fucker. Mother-son-of-a-whore fucker."

Hanna swallowed and stared out the windshield at Jalyn's house. It was pretty. Tan siding with a darker brick front on it. The landscaping was lush and thriving. Jalyn and her mom spent hours outside working on it. A lump grew in her throat. There'd been a day when she had a cute little house like this, back in Colorado. She'd spent so much time making it the perfect home for Isaac and herself.

"So, now what?" Jalyn softly asked. Her hand reached over and gripped Hanna's. They sat quietly in her SUV. It was still running, so they had air conditioning.

"She says she's going to find a lawyer who will agree with her that I'm partially to blame, so she gets some of her money back from me."

Jalyn shrugged. "She won't. She's mad. Lashing out. But, frankly, she freely gave it without checking out who that jackass was. There isn't a lawyer out there who won't see that."

Hanna nodded and frowned. "Yeah."

"How did this woman get your number?"

"I don't know. I didn't ask because, honestly, I didn't want to engage her further in conversation. I was stunned stupid and didn't want to say the wrong thing."

Jalyn nodded. "What about your money?"

"The bank is making me whole because they have an admission from the redhead."

"That's a start."

Hanna nodded. "Yeah, and they are doing a forensic audit to see if there's more. Their insurance will cover anything I lost."

"Okay." Jalyn inhaled a deep breath and blew it out in a whoosh. "That bastard makes me so fucking mad."

"I know. Me too."

"You need to tell your dad."

"I know. Thank goodness he's the bakery's money manager. I'm going to ask him to be a second on my bank account so he can watch to make sure Isaac isn't figuring out another way to get to my account."

"That's a great idea."

"And, I have a date tonight, but I think I'm going to cancel."

Jalyn whipped around in her seat and faced her. "Say what?"

"Date."

"With who?"

She took a deep breath and let it out slowly. "Quinn Kurtz."

"Oh, lordy, he's as hot as they come." Jalyn fanned herself with her hand. "I wondered when he'd start dating again. That ex of his gave him a run for his money. She threw every stone she could at him. She threatened all sorts of bad things, and tried telling everyone in town he was terrible. That he hit her and treated her badly. Just to make herself look like the victim. But he handled it with grace and dignity. Kept his nose to the grindstone and worked." Jalyn grinned. "He asked you out?"

"I can't go."

"The hell you can't. Why on earth not?"

"He's charming."

"And the issue with that?"

"Isaac was charming."

"They are NOT the same kind of charming. Isaac is smarmy and sneaky and charming, so he can get something. Quinn is a southern gentleman, charming and raised right. He's raised his kids right too. They're both upstanding people."

She stared into her friend's green eyes. Her dark ponytail was still perched high on her head. "But..."

"No buts. Quinn Kurtz is an absolute *yes*, Hanna. If you're talking to me to see if I'm going to talk you out of it, I am not."

Quinn walked across the beach and pointed to markers in the sand. He looked at Jared and the couple of guys with him from his crew.

"Okay, we're starting here. The stage is going to be this way. We want it to be slightly situated so that it partially faces the beach but also partially faces the crowd sitting on the sand. I've got the markers set. We should be ready to go. A load of lumber will come in later on today. I had it ordered for another job that's now been cancelled. Jace must have a fairy godmother or something to be so damned lucky. I'll have them drop it over there." He pointed to an area between the soon-to-be stage, and the parking lot. "So right now, set the footings and start the frame. Square it on the ground and then we'll lift it tomorrow once the cement dries. Questions?"

Jared and the guys all shook their heads no.

He grinned and nodded. "All right. I'll be back later. I'm going to go check on another job."

He felt happy.

He felt excited.

He felt buoyant.

He felt good about his date tonight. It had been a long damn time. A long damn time since he'd had a date. And he was ready.

Hopping in his truck, he decided to swing past Miracle Garage and see if Sid was about. As soon as he pulled into the parking area, Sid looked up from the car he was working on. Cooper Lucht, who used to own the garage, was only seen from his ass down. He was bent over under the hood of a car. It looked almost comical. Like a pair of stuffed bib overalls just to make it look like the garage was busy.

"Hey, what are you doing here?"

Quinn chuckled, shook his friend's hand, and gave him a quick slap on the back, in a half man hug.

"I thought I'd stop by. I've got a crew building a stage over at Jace's for my party and then obviously for afterward. But I just thought I'd come and check in. I haven't seen you for any length of time recently."

Sid nodded and grinned. "Yeah, been busy here, but hey, Grace and I set a wedding date. We're getting married in a month. Gonna keep it small. Friends only. Hope you'll attend. Kind of expecting you to be my best man."

Quinn grinned broadly. "I'd be happy to be your best man. What about Jace?"

"He's my best man, too. I'm gonna have two, cause I can't really do it without you guys."

Quinn nodded. "That sounds about right. Anything else we're gonna have to do on your wedding day?"

Sid laughed. "No."

Quinn nodded and rocked back on his heels. "So, I have a date tonight."

Sid's eyes rounded. He stared at his friend for a long time. Quinn squirmed a little bit under the scrutiny.

"You have a date?"

"Yeah. Yeah, I have a date. Hanna Valentine from the bakery."

Sid chuckled. "Yeah, the cinnamon roll woman. Damn, she knows how to make an excellent cinnamon roll. Grace has been feeding me those for a couple weeks now."

He patted his stomach. "I'm gonna be fat before the wedding. Hope she knows what she's getting into with this."

Quinn laughed. "Yeah, Jared's pretty hooked on those cinnamon rolls, too. I have to admit they are good."

Sid nodded. "They sure as hell are. So you got a date with her. I can't believe it. How long has it been?"

"Yeah. I have a date. It kind of came about by accident. She was bringing fresh bread into Jace's this morning when I was there, and I don't know." He shrugged and looked at the blacktop beneath his feet. "It just kind of came out of my mouth."

Sid laughed. "Yeah, I remember that. When I met Grace, it was like my mouth had a mind of its own. Things came out of my mouth. I didn't expect to come out."

Quinn nodded. "Yeah, that's kind of what I mean."

"So, what are you gonna do? Where are you gonna take her?"

Quinn shrugged. "Shit, I haven't even thought of that. I suppose I'll just take her to the Sandbar."

Sid shook his head. "That's lame. Don't take her there. Not that there's anything wrong with the Sandbar, and don't tell Jace I said that. But you won't be able to talk while you're there. Everybody in town knows you. They'll be stopping to talk. Unless that's what you're looking for."

Quinn shrugged. "I don't know what I'm looking for. I guess not that, though. I'd like to spend time talking to get to know her."

"That's what I'm saying. So take her out to the Supper Club."

"Oh, that's a good idea. Okay." He thought a moment, then nodded. "Yep." Inhaling a deep breath, he let it out in a whoosh. "I'm nervous. Can you tell?"

Sid laughed. "Yes, I can tell. But I remember it well. I was where you were not long ago. But that first date with Grace, that was the best thing that ever happened to me."

"Well, I'm not looking to get married or anything. I just kind of miss the female company, you know?"

Sid laughed. "I do know. I do know exactly. Enjoy it. She's a good girl. I don't know much about her."

"From what I understand, she had moved out of town after high school, went to college, and never came back until recently, I guess about a month ago or something. Her mom ran the bakery all this time. But I think what I heard was she can't handle it anymore, Mom I mean. So Hanna came back and is running the bakery now."

"That sounds about right, I guess, from the little things I've been hearing. Okay. Well, let me know what I have to wear for the wedding. And I'll let you know how the date goes."

Sid chuckled. "It'll go fine. Be yourself. You're a great guy, Quinn. One of my best friends. I want only the best for you. If Hanna is as smart as I'm hearing, she'll see that and know it too."

9

Hanna finished up the dishes in the bakery, and ran to grab her little floral overnight bag that she'd packed clean clothes in. Hurrying to the bathroom, she freshened up, added a little bit of lip gloss and some mascara, and nervously inspected herself in the mirror. It's good. She's good. It's all good.

She brushed her hair out, letting it fall over her shoulders, and headed into the kitchen to dry the dishes she'd just washed.

After putting everything away, she wiped down the counter and held her stomach one more time as nerves made her a little queasy.

Hearing a truck outside, she twisted her fingers together as she stepped to the front door.

Opening the door for Quinn, she smiled as he stepped inside. "You look beautiful."

His aftershave wrapped around her and for a moment, she could only think of how great he smelled. "Thank you." The heat crawled up her chest and landed in her cheeks.

"You look very handsome yourself."

He shook his head and smiled. "I wasn't fishing for a compliment."

"I know." She quietly responded, feeling a bit sheepish now.

She watched Quinn peruse the bakery. She couldn't tell from the expression on his face what he thought about it. Then again, he was here yesterday and had seen it. "Your bakery is nice. I like the ambiance. It's warm and inviting."

She glanced around to see what he was seeing. "Thank you. It's probably in need of an update soon enough. I think my mom updated this place probably twenty years ago now, and since then only just little things here and there as they were needed. But honestly, I haven't decided yet what I want to do with it, and I'm still getting my feet wet with running the bakery."

"That's right. You're back in town from being somewhere else, correct?"

"Yes, I was in Colorado, Denver area. Ah, for the last twenty years or so. I went there for college, got married, and I managed a large restaurant while I was there. I had these big pie-in-the-sky dreams of being some huge popular master chef. But the business is hard, and my mom's health isn't the best. Arthritis has crept in, and she had a hard time manning the bakery. When I got divorced, she asked me to come back and take over the bakery from her. It had been the family dream all along." She swallowed. "I'll say I reluctantly came back, but it was good for the break, change in scenery, and a fresh start. So here I am, making my cinnamon rolls, trying to keep Grandma's recipes going, and figuring out what I want to do with my business and my bakery."

She watched Quinn's face as his eyes landed on the tables and the counter and the chalkboard behind the back bar where she wrote down the daily specials. It wasn't a bad bakery. It just needed updating. And she wasn't embarrassed that he was looking it over. And he wasn't bad to look at, anyway. But she still felt a bit nervous.

He said, "Well, there's time for all of that. When you know what you want, it'll be time. Until then, keep baking those cinnamon rolls. I have a crew full of guys that absolutely love them. And I say that sheepishly because I love them, too."

She chuckled, "Thank you. I really do appreciate that."

"Shall we go?"

"Sure. Let me just make sure the back door's locked, please."

She hustled to the kitchen, locked the back door, checked things over, and was happy with the way everything looked and would be ready for tomorrow.

And then she hurried to the front. "Okay, all set," she said.

Quinn turned and smiled at her, then opened the door to the bakery and held it open for her. She pulled her keys from her little shoulder bag and he held his hand out.

"I can do it."

She was flustered. Her fingers shook a little bit. "Sure."

Wow, it had been years since a man had offered to do something so mundane for her.

He locked the bakery door for her, and then with his hand at the small of her back, he walked her around to the passenger side of his truck.

Butterflies swarmed her stomach as she felt his firm warm hand at her back.

She was excited. She was nervous. She was all the things.

He opened the passenger door and a drop-down running board lowered itself.

He held his hand out and she gently placed her palm against his as she lifted herself up onto the running board. Electricity shot up her arm as their palms touched. His skin was warm. His hand was firm and slightly rough from his construction work.

Hers were much different. She worked with cookie and bread dough all day. Her hands were soft.

She sat inside, tugging on her tan skort to make sure she wasn't showing more than was appropriate. Buckling her seat belt, she watched as Quinn walked around the front of the truck.

She inhaled his aftershave as it lingered in the truck. A little thrill ran through her. Woodsy. Maybe a little spicy. He smelled fantastic.

Quinn climbed into the truck and said, "I thought we'd go out to the Supper Club. Have you been there since you've been back?"

She swallowed. "Actually, I've never been there. It wasn't here when I left town twenty years ago."

"Didn't you get back to see your parents?"

"Now and then, but we come from a cooking family, so we didn't go out to eat much. And Dad likes to grill now and then, so he would man the grill when I came back. He said his ladies needed to relax from cooking and let him help us, and take care of us. We were always happy to oblige." She smiled.

Quinn chuckled, and it was nice. She liked the way he laughed. His face transformed when he smiled. He was very handsome.

He maneuvered the truck out of the parking lot, around the square, and down Main Street, making a left on Main Street and turning down on Second Street. At the end of Second Street was the Supper Club, across from the police station.

He pulled into the parking lot and hopped out quickly. She reached for the door handle and then realized she was supposed to wait. She'd forgotten what this was like. Isaac had never opened the door for her or showed her chivalry. It was foreign to her, all the social graces. She waited for him to open the door, feeling a little foolish. She could open it herself, but he was being a gentleman, and she was going to let him.

He opened the door and held his hand out for her, and those little butterflies began fluttering around her belly again. They walked into the restaurant, Quinn's hand at the small of her back. It made her feel taken care of and revered. Wasn't that silly? A simple gesture like his hand at the small of her back gave her goosebumps.

She quickly shook her head to change the trajectory of her thoughts. This was just a date among friends, new friends, nothing more. She didn't need anything more right now. She wasn't even sure what was going to happen with all of the stuff with Isaac.

They were seated at a table. People looked their way. A lot of people in town knew Quinn.

"Hello, Quinn. How are you?" They greeted.

He responded to everyone nicely. "May I introduce you to Hanna Valentine? Hanna owns the bakery. Mae's."

People seemed happy to meet her, and she wondered how soon before word would get around to everyone in town that she had a date with Quinn Kurtz.

She chuckled. "Small towns are interesting."

Quinn grinned as they settled in their seats. "So tell me about Hanna Valentine," he asked.

She let out a breath. "Well, let's see. I graduated top of my class from the culinary school in Boulder, Colorado. I started a job at a restaurant shortly after graduation. I had worked there part-time while I was in college. I had every intention of being the head chef there, but that wasn't meant to be, I guess. It's a very tough industry, and especially in some of the prime restaurants. You really have to have a lot of experience and work your way up. I started as a garde-manager. That's a pantry chef. I worked my way up to commis chef, which means I followed the chef around to learn. He'd give me tasks, and I'd have to prove myself. Then I made it to pastry chef, and that's where I excelled and stayed.

"Unfortunately for me, I'm great with desserts. I guess that's fortunate now that I have the bakery. But unfortunately, at the time, it appeared I was too good, and they had no intention of moving me off of desserts.

"And then I got divorced, and Mom needed help at the bakery and asked me to come back. So I guess it was meant to be. How about you, Quinn Kurtz? What about you?"

He chuckled. It was a beautiful sound coming from deep in his chest. It was genuine. His smile was beautiful. His dark eyes landed on hers.

And he said, "Well, Quinn Kurtz went into the service after high school. And when I got out, I came back and started my construction company. I've always been good with building, and I've always been great with my hands. And I decided that's what I wanted to do. You know, after a few years of kicking around in between times, starting a construction business in a small town isn't easy. But I was born and raised here. My parents had a lot of contacts. And slowly, but surely, I managed to get little jobs here and there. I struggle a bit with PTSD. I've mostly managed to keep it under control. And my way of giving back is that I only hire veterans. As a matter of fact, my son Jared, went into the service so he could get hired by me. That's how serious I am about it. And I'm proud of that."

She nodded. "That's wonderful. Thank you so much for your service and for hiring veterans."

"My pleasure," he said. "Did you serve?"

"No, I'm afraid I didn't. I went right to culinary school from high school. I've often wondered if I should have when I've seen men and women come back. They stand taller and prouder for having served, despite the hidden injuries."

"Well," he said, "not everybody serves. And as long as you keep serving those wonderful baked goods of yours, we're all good."

She chuckled. Butterflies swirled in her tummy as she watched his genuine interest in her. He was intent and didn't let those walking by their table divert his attention. It was refreshing.

"So what's next for Quinn Kurtz? Do you have big projects lined up?"

He leaned back and smiled. "Yes, right now we are building a stage, believe it or not, at Sarge's for..."

He chuckled, "Well, I guess it's for Jace. He likes to have live music there, here and there, but he wants to have it more often. I'm having a big party there in three weeks. It's actually a celebration of me not having to pay alimony anymore. And I'm in touch with Jami Hart from Hart & the Hurricanes. It appears that they'll be in town for my party and have agreed to play. Therefore, Jace has commissioned a stage at the bar outside on the sand. So that's what we're in the middle of building right now."

He took a drink of water and she watched his Adam's apple move up and down. "And just this morning, I put an offer in to buy the Army barracks just outside of town."

"Oh, that's wonderful. I've seen that old installation and thought someone should do something with it. It's looking rather rough. What will you do with that?"

"I'm thinking apartments. Maybe condos."

She grinned at him. "Have you thought about making it housing for veterans working for you? Veterans coming to town? Veteran housing is so needed."

He looked at her, his brows furrowed, and he cocked his head to the side. He leaned his forearms on the table. "Hanna, that is the best idea I've heard all day. Thank you so much for thinking of that. And you're right. I hire these guys, sometimes fresh out of the military, and they don't have a place to stay. I think that's just what I'm going to do. Thank you so much for the idea."

She swallowed a knot that formed in her throat. Hopefully, she didn't steer him in the wrong direction. "Please don't do it on my account. What if I'm wrong?"

He shook his head. "You're not wrong. You're absolutely right. And I love the idea."

Their food came, and they ate. Small talk. He told her about Jared and his service, and that he was going to make him the assistant general contractor on the Army barracks job. He felt so much better about having a firm direction to go with that.

She told him about her mom and her dad.

The conversation floated briefly to Isaac when Quinn asked, "So, is your ex in town?"

"No, he's not in town, and I'm grateful for that, but I still seem to have to clean up some of his messes."

Quinn shook his head. "I know what you mean. My ex has been a pain all these five years after our divorce. It's always something new with her. She continues to find ways to drag me into something. But I'm officially finished with that."

Hanna nodded. "I'm hoping to get there soon. I don't want to deal with any more of his messes. He keeps getting in trouble. He's been trouble from day one."

Quinn grinned. "How about we both make a deal with each other? We're both finished cleaning up our ex's messes."

She laughed. "I love that idea. Deal."

She reached across the table and they shook hands. That same electric bolt ran up her arm. His skin was warm, his handshake firm, and he stared right into her eyes. That was the most disconcerting. His eyes were wonderful, dark, shiny, and captivating. She had to be very careful around this man.

The waitress stopped at their table. "Did you folks save room for dessert?"

He conspiratorially leaned forward and said, "Though I doubt that you'd want anyone else's dessert since you're the expert on desserts and all. But would you like something else?"

The waitress inhaled. "Oh my God, that's who you are. You're Hanna from Mae's."

Hanna chuckled, "Yes, I'm from Mae's. And no, thank you. I didn't save room for dessert."

Quinn grinned, "I'll pass myself. Thank you. I'll just take the check."

The waitress hustled off and came back very soon with

the check, took their plates, and Quinn said, "Thank you for a lovely dinner, Hanna. It's been a long time since I've been able to enjoy the company of a beautiful woman. And I'm grateful you said yes."

She felt the heat climb up her torso and her cheeks warmed. "Thank you for asking. I nearly called to cancel today, but I'm glad I didn't."

"That would have been a travesty. We both deserve some respite from our former lives."

Quinn pulled Hanna's chair out for her and followed her to the front of the restaurant. He liked keeping his hand at the small of her back. The connection to a beautiful woman felt great. He truly had forgotten what a pleasure it could be to spend time with someone who didn't want something from you. She was smart and interesting. Yes, he'd missed this.

As they exited the restaurant, Hanna's phone rang. She pulled it from her bag, glanced at the screen, and dropped it back into her bag.

"Please answer it if you need to. I won't be offended."

She smiled, but it didn't reach her eyes. "I didn't recognize the number. Likely a scammer, so I'll pass for now."

He helped her into the truck. The simple touch of her hand was thrilling. This was how his father taught him to treat a woman. Make her feel special and cared for, and he loved how he felt being a gentleman. As he climbed into the truck once more, Hanna's phone rang.

Her smile was forced. "I'm sorry. I'll just turn it off."

He shook his head. "No need. I'm surprised my phone hasn't interrupted us this evening. Usually, that's when I get a handful of calls. People inquiring about their remodel jobs or timing of things or questions about the job. Tonight, the universe must have muted my phone!"

She chuckled. "The universe didn't get that order to my phone."

He grinned and backed them out of the parking lot. As he began driving toward Mae's, her phone rang once more.

He glanced quickly at her and laughed. "Someone needs to speak with you."

Her full lips turned down in a slight frown and she finally answered her pesky phone. "Hello, this is Hanna?"

He watched as her face changed to one of concern. Her pretty brows furrowed. "I'm not responsible for Isaac's finances. You'll need to take it up with him."

She ended the call and shut her phone off. Her hands dropped into her lap and he felt bad for her. "Some of the crap you're still dealing with?"

Her eyes landed on his. "Yes. It's been a particularly bad week."

He nodded. "I'm sorry."

"It isn't your responsibility to be sorry. My dad will help me with this stuff and I'm going to do my best to not worry about Isaac and his many, many issues."

He chuckled. "See? That's what I'm talking about. The past is simply something we had to endure to get to the present."

She smiled. "I love that. That's going to be my mantra from this point forward."

Rather than turn onto the square, he asked, "Do you have your car in the back?"

"Yes. Thank you."

He turned onto the alley, which was named, Alley, and swept around the corner, pulling in next to Hanna's car. He'd made the decision earlier today that this was simply a first date. A chance for them to get to know each other. He was going to walk her to her car and bid farewell. No awkward first kiss.

He stepped out of his truck and hustled around to the passenger side. He smiled as he held his hand out. Her blue eyes were captivating. Such a deep blue framed in thick dark lashes. She was stunning. Her hair flowed around her shoulders in waves, framing a face that could grace any magazine cover or billboard. He didn't think she even knew how attractive she was. Maybe that was part of the appeal.

He helped her down from his truck. She pulled her keys from her purse and clicked the button on the fob and her car doors unlocked with a click.

He opened her driver's door and grinned. "It was a pleasure spending time with you. I do hope you'll join me again soon."

She seemed genuinely happy there'd be no awkwardness and smiled one of the prettiest smiles he'd seen on any human ever. "I would be happy to do so and thank you very much for dinner and great conversation."

She hesitated only a millisecond, then slid into the driver's seat of her SUV. He closed her door, nodded, and walked around to the driver's side of his truck. His chest puffed with pride as he climbed into his truck. It was a wonderful date. He was the perfect gentleman and the dawning of his next thought slightly surprised him. He wanted to have another date with Hanna Valentine. He wanted to spend time talking to her. He'd give it a day or so and stop in the bakery and ask her out again.

Hanna pulled away from the bakery. He then did the same but decided to stop in at the Sandbar and have a drink. Maybe things would have settled a bit and Jace had a moment to chat with him.

As he pulled into Sarge's, he noted the parking lot was full. Chances were Jace was busy, but he'd have a drink and check on the footings for the stage that had been set today. As he marched across the sand, he saw the freshly dug sand in piles and inspected the job his crew had done today. It looked wonderful, and the stage was going to be fantastic. Jace would have this place hopping every single night. Not that it wasn't already, but he'd triple his income with nightly music.

"It looks good. I'm already booking entertainment." Jace's voice called out.

He turned to see his friend walking toward him with a huge smile on his face. "I'm happy to hear that. There's nothing sadder than an empty stage."

Jace laughed. "It won't be empty long. But your party is the first. We'll have a stage opening and having Hart & the Hurricanes as the first band to grace the stage is perfect. Hometown band gone big, right here to inaugurate my new stage."

Quinn nodded. "I can't wait for the day." He glanced to the side. "I'm glad the lumber arrived. We'll get this baby up as soon as the cement footings allow."

Jace nudged him. "How was your date?"

Quinn grinned. "It was a great date. Just getting to

know each other. Delicious food, great company. A nice date."

Jace slapped him on the back. "Good to hear. Need a drink?"

"Yep. I'll buy."

11

Hanna sighed deeply as she drove from behind the bakery. It had been a nice date. It had been a long time since she'd been on a nice date. Deciding she needed to deal with this Isaac thing sooner rather than later, she glanced at her watch and noticed it was still only eight o'clock.

Turning toward her parents' house, she navigated the darkening streets, streetlights beginning to flicker on as she drove. Her mind was all over the place. Don't get involved with Quinn, get involved with Quinn, don't get involved. He's too charming. Things are messy right now.

Her mind was all over the place and gosh she was just freshly new in town and was still trying to get her bearings at the bakery. It was a silly time to try to get involved with anyone. But she really liked him. He was, well, he was a gentleman.

He was handsome, so incredibly handsome, and smart and gosh he ran his own business and he ran it well, something Isaac never did. Isaac was always scamming people. That was his business, actually. He was a professional scammer.

Why didn't she see it sooner? She pulled into her parents' driveway and noticed the lights were still on. She sighed deeply and hefted herself out of the car. She suddenly felt ten years older. The weight of Isaac and his shit sat heavily on her. As she sauntered toward the front door, the porch light clicked, and she saw her dad peek out the window.

Before she made it to the front door, it opened. "Hey baby girl, come on in. What's going on?"

She hesitated a moment, stepped in, and gave her dad a big hug. "Do you and Mom have a minute? I know it's late, but I need to speak with you about something."

His gray brows furrowed, and he stared into her eyes for a while. "Of course, we always have time for you honey. Come on in."

She moved into the living room where her mother sat, concern already on her face. Her mom stood and edged toward her. Wrapping her arms around her mom, she heard her whisper. "I was hoping you'd tell us something sooner or later. I could tell today something wasn't right."

Hanna chuckled. "You know me so well, but I thought this was something I could handle. I guess I need reinforcements and maybe some help."

She sat on the sofa next to her mom. Her dad sat in a chair across the coffee table from them. He leaned his elbows on his knees, folded his hands together, and looked her in the eye.

"The best way to do it is to peel the band-aid off girl." Hanna nodded and swallowed. "I know."

She sighed. "So Isaac pulled another fun scam and I've got some women trying to involve me in it."

Her father's glance to her mother didn't go unnoticed, but Hanna kept telling her story.

"It appears Isaac has been catfishing women."

Her mother turned to her. "What does that mean?"

"Catfishing, you know, pretending to be someone on the internet, promising them the moon, 'I'm going to marry you, I'm rich, I'm starting a new business, I just need a little bit of money.'

"Etcetera, etcetera. He got these women to send him money. And two of them have now found me and are planning on suing me to get all their money back or at least some of it."

Her father shook his head, "Well that's not going to go anywhere. You're legally divorced, so it doesn't matter. They can try to sue all they want to."

"I know, Dad, but it appears that he was catfishing them while we were still married. The second lady, who called today, told me it took her two years to find me. That would have made me married to Isaac at the time. I don't know what will happen with this. I don't know what the legal ramifications are."

Her father said, "Well, we'll talk to our attorney, Grant Park, tomorrow. You can come into his office with me, and we're going to sit down and talk this out and see what he thinks. I think if you can prove that you've never touched that money; and quite frankly, if Isaac was getting money from these women, where was he putting it? Did he have a private bank account? That would be the best thing. Then we could prove that you never touched it. Even for things like paying the house payment or car payments or any marital expenses. So if we can prove that he had a separate bank account, that's the best thing."

She took a deep breath. Could it be that simple? "Well,

he had to have a separate bank account, Dad, because I had my own account. We had a joint account that we each deposited money into every month to pay expenses like the house payment and any repairs on the house. And then he had his own account, which I assume is where he was putting the money unless he also had a second separate account."

"How did he deposit money into that joint account?"

"His employer direct deposited it."

Her father nodded. "Well, that's good to know. That certainly keeps the lines clearer between you and these women."

Hanna picked at a piece of lint on her skort. "Okay, so the other thing I didn't tell you about, but am confessing now, is that Isaac had sweet-talked the redhead at the bank into giving him access to my account. He told her that I stole from him and he just wanted his money back. She drained my account for him and transferred the money over to his account electronically. I spoke to the bank this week. I found out when I went to the thrift store to buy the bathroom vanity. The bank is making me whole. They fired the redhead and they are setting things in place to make sure this doesn't happen to anyone ever again."

Her father leaned back in his chair. "Shit."

Hanna's mom reached over, picked up her hand, and held it tightly. "But what I'd like for you to do, Dad, is take over or be a second on my bank account so that you can watch it more regularly than I do. With just getting my feet wet in the bakery right now, I don't have time to check my bank account every day. And I need somebody else to help me watch over it."

Her father's soft smile warmed her heart. "Honey, we

would do anything for you and I absolutely will do everything in my power to make sure Isaac Annen doesn't ever get a red cent from you again. As for these women, tomorrow we're going to go talk to Grant. We're going to figure out how we can protect you from these women. They shouldn't even be allowed to contact you. So we'll put a stop to that, and we'll set things in place to protect you from any more women coming out of the woodwork and harassing you."

Her mom squeezed her hand again. Her father rubbed his chin with his fingers. "It's a shame. You married yourself one piece of work there, but I'm so glad you're not married to him anymore. It makes us rest easier knowing that he's not out there scamming you or getting you involved in his gambling and ridiculous games. I tell you, it broke our hearts seeing you work so hard to pay off cars that he'd gambled away because you had loans on them. We were so worried. I'm glad those times are over."

"Me too, Dad. Me too." She repeated. "I was so stupid not to see him for what he was before."

Her mom let go of her hand and patted her knee. "Young love. We've all been there."

Her mom's eyes swiveled to her dad's, and she smiled. Then she looked back at Hanna.

"But you have to look at the best parts of this. You've learned valuable lessons. You'll never go through anything like that again. And you know we always have your back."

"Thanks, Mom." Her mom hugged her and kissed her on the top of the head. And Hanna's heart felt so much more at peace, knowing she had these people in her corner. They were her strength throughout her whole life and certainly when she was dealing with Isaac's messes.

They bolstered her up. They never helped her financially, though. They made her work her way out of it. She used to be irritated by that, but now she understood what they were trying to do. They wanted her to make the decision herself to get rid of Isaac.

And while she had married not to get unmarried, she had tried so hard to make that one work.

But she'd never be so gullible again. That was a fact.

Quinn left his house with a lighter step than he had yesterday. They had a nice date last night. And he wanted to ask her out again. Boy, it was great sitting and having adult company and looking into those blue eyes of hers. That was no hardship at all.

Deciding to stop at the bakery and buy his crew cinnamon rolls would do two things for him. It would make him a well-loved boss today, feeding his workers something sweet, and he'd get to see Hanna.

He turned his truck into the parking lot and hopped out with a step so light he could have skipped. As he entered the bakery, the warmth and the aromas of those cinnamon rolls and freshly baked bread and...was that pumpkin bread he smelled? Oh, he had a weakness for pumpkin bread.

He looked at the bakery-filled case and felt relief. There were people standing in line ahead of him, but there should be enough left for his needs.

Hanna came out from the kitchen with a bag in her

hand. She hadn't seen him yet. He was standing behind an old fella he recognized from the hardware store.

She smiled brightly and breezed. "There you go, Mrs. Howell. I added a couple extra little goodies in there for you. You all have a nice women's meeting this morning."

Mrs. Howell nodded and said sweetly, "Oh, we always have a nice meeting, Hanna. And these goodies here will help make it extra sweet. Thank you."

Mrs. Howell paid for her order and walked past the people in line and out the door. The next person in line asked for a dozen cookies and a cinnamon roll.

Hanna breezed over to the case and deftly opened a bag. "Do you know which cookies you want?"

The young man at the counter said, "Yes, I want six of the chocolate ones and six of those sugar cookies."

"You got it." Hanna quickly filled the bag, added his cinnamon roll, wrapped in a separate little sheet of bakery paper on the top, rolled the top of the bag closed, and checked him out.

When she looked up at the man in front of him, she finally noticed him. Her smile was bright, and genuine, and sexy.

He grinned and nodded, and she faltered a little bit. She stumbled on her words, "Hi, Mr. ...Trask. How can I help you today?"

Quinn put his head down and looked at his shoes. A grin spread on his face. She kind of affected him that way too, and wasn't that nice?

Mr. Trask placed his order. She deftly fulfilled it, rang him up, and then it was finally his turn.

"How are you today?" He asked her.

She smiled, "I'm doing well. How are you?"

"I'm eager to repeat what we did last night. I'd love to have dinner with you again."

She smiled, "I'd like that too."

She glanced around to make sure that no one was listening. There were people sitting at tables, and no one was standing in line behind him, but she lowered her voice. "I still have this mess going on with my ex. I just feel a little conflicted about getting involved when I've got all this going on."

He leaned in so he could lower his voice as well. "Well, I don't know if having a couple dinners is getting involved, but I'd still like to have dinner with you. And I thought we agreed not to dwell on our ex's messes, remember?"

She chuckled, "You're right. We did say that."

"What's it going to hurt? Let's go to the Sandbar. We'll sit on the beach tonight. We'll have something light to eat, maybe a drink or two, and just talk."

Her eyes met his. "Well, yes, that sounds nice, actually. Thank you."

"I'll pick you up at home."

She cleared her throat, and he watched her cheeks turn pink. "How about here? I normally work until the evening, anyway, getting ready for the next day. And I'll be honest with you. My place is a mess. I've been remodeling and I just... it's not fit for company."

His hand flew over his heart. "Ouch! You're remodeling and you didn't have me look at it?"

She laughed. "Well, I didn't have anybody look at it. I'm actually doing it myself."

He shook his head. "You're remodeling yourself. So you bake these wonderful cinnamon rolls and you can remodel a house?"

"Well, I don't know how good I am at it, but I'm trying.

Again, money, my ex, and all that. So I just found it necessary to have to do some things on my own."

Quinn nodded. "It's all right. I can see that it's maybe too soon for that conversation. So how about this? I'll pick you up here. Will six-thirty work?"

Her cheeks turned an adorable pink. He saw a color tint under her chin and in the "V" of her blue t-shirt.

"Yes, six-thirty will be fine. Thank you for understanding."

He nodded. "You know, I've been in situations similar to what you're in, where money was tight and things just had to be done on a shoestring. I'm still open to helping you, but I'm not going to push."

She smiled. "Thank you. I do appreciate it. It won't be forever. And I'm actually getting a lot of satisfaction out of doing things on my own. I'm learning that I'm pretty darn capable."

He chuckled. "I have no doubt, Hanna Valentine. I have no doubt."

"Okay," she half giggled. "What can I get for you this morning?"

He smiled, "I'd like a dozen of your cinnamon rolls, and I need six coffees to go, please. I'm treating the crew."

Her smile grew wide, and he thought she was the loveliest woman he'd seen in, well, forever. She was adorable with those dimples. She was beautiful inside and out.

"You're going to be popular at work today," she replied cheerfully, as she deftly pulled the cinnamon rolls out of the case and lined them up in a box.

She closed the box with nimble fingers, grabbed a tray for the coffees, and slowly filled the six cups, pushing them into the little slots in the tray to hold them in place.

She tapped lids on top. When she looked at him, she asked, "Do you need cream and sugar?"

He shrugged. "You know, I guess this is bad of me, but I don't know. So let's just say yes, just in case."

She chuckled, "No worries. I'll add enough for everyone, just in case."

She bagged things up for him, putting the cream and sugar in a separate little bag with some stir sticks, and then she rang up his order.

He paid quickly with his credit card and then he winked at her. "I'll see you at six-thirty, Hanna Valentine."

She nodded and those cute pink cheeks brightened. "I'll see you at six-thirty, Quinn Kurtz."

13

anna's morning flew by. Customers came in steadily. And her baked goods were coming out of the oven perfectly.

Her mom stopped in for a little while, around ten-thirty, and helped her get the case refilled. She did a few miscellaneous things in the kitchen. And Hanna always appreciated that so much.

"I really do thank you, for doing the dishes, Mom."

Her mom chuckled. "It's all right, dear. The warm water helps my hands feel a little bit better. So I don't mind doing them at all. And besides, you're doing a fantastic job here, and I love watching that. And this gives me a little something to do, but not on a schedule. So it works out perfectly. Also, I can be here when your dad takes you over to see Grant today."

"Thank you, Mom. Daddy said he would be here at three o'clock, so you don't have to stay the whole afternoon. But if you want to come back with him, I sure would appreciate it. That way, I don't have to close the doors.

And I'll have some bread in the oven that you can pull out by then."

"Sounds good, honey. Now you go on out and do what you need to do. I'm fine here in the kitchen."

The bell over the door rang, and Hanna hurried out to see who had come in. And there stood Tisha.

Hanna hadn't seen her since that day at the thrift store.

She had those light green eyes, those thick dark lashes. Her hair was cut in such a severe, bob. Straight bangs, and then straight to just below her ears. The light color of her hair did nothing to soften the look.

It was severe looking and she couldn't help but think that Tisha would probably look more welcoming with a softer haircut.

But she seemed to like this aloof and unapproachable demeanor she wore. Maybe it was her armor. Maybe after getting a divorce, she needed something to make her feel empowered and maybe her hairstyle was it.

"Hi, Tisha. How can I help you today?"

"Well, I actually came by to see if you'd like to come to my place for lunch. I have some flooring I'd like you to look at. I have it left over, and I wondered if it would work for your house. And I would like you to see a couple pieces of furniture that I'm ready to get rid of in case you need them."

"Oh, wow. That's really so sweet of you. Thank you so much. I don't want you to feel like I'm a charity case or anything. It was just a mix-up at the thrift store."

Tisha shook her head and held her hand up. "No worries. I don't think you're a charity case. My son loves your cinnamon rolls, by the way, and talks about them all the time. And I remember meeting you and thinking that we are in somewhat of the same situation. Both of us divorced. Both of us have exes that leave a lot to be desired, if that can be said."

Hanna chuckled. "That can be said. That's actually the nicest thing that could be said."

Tisha nodded. "Perfect. Can I expect you at noon? I'll have something made, although it probably won't be nearly as delicious as what you can make. But I will have lunch so that you can eat. I can show you the flooring and the kitchen table that I have. And I have a couple of other little, small things, and then I'll let you get back to work."

Hanna swallowed. "Thank you, Tisha. That's really very nice. I'll see if my mom can watch the bakery for me for about a half hour. Would that be enough time? I'm not even sure where you live, to be honest."

Tisha's smile crawled across her face. It was almost a little eerie. "I don't live far out of town."

She pulled out a sheet of paper and a pen from her purse, and she scribbled down her address, then handed it to Hanna.

"I have a sign out front that says, 'Home of the Barkley's.' Once you see that sign, you know you're at the right place. It'll only take you about five minutes to get out there. So don't worry about having to leave for too much time, and I will see you at noon."

"Thank you so much, Tisha. Thank you."

She swallowed. If her mom couldn't watch the bakery, maybe Jalyn could come over for a half hour. She watched Tisha's straight, rigid actually, back as she retreated. She almost glided across the floor and out the door.

She climbed into a Lexus, not the pickup truck she drove the other day.

Hanna sighed. Tisha Barkley was way out of her league. What was she even doing, having lunch with her?

It seemed like they were on two very different playing fields. But maybe she needed a friend. So Hanna would go. She stepped into the kitchen and saw her mom putting the pans away.

"Mom, are you able to watch the bakery around noon for half an hour? I've been invited to lunch."

"Oh, a date?"

"Well, not a date, like *date date*. It's a lady that I met at the thrift store the other night. She was actually bringing a beautiful bathroom vanity in to sell when I was trying to buy mine. And she gave it to me. And she stopped in just now. She wants to have lunch with me. So I thought I would go."

"Oh, honey, that's really nice. Yes, of course. I can make time to watch the bakery for you. I love seeing you getting out and being social. Now, if you only could find a nice man to have a date with."

Hanna's cheeks burned brightly. She wasn't ready to tell her mom about Quinn. I mean, what could she tell her, anyway? They were just having their second dinner together. And that was it. They hadn't even kissed. So there was really nothing to tell her. And she sure didn't want to get her hopes up. My goodness, she was so excited for her to be with anyone other than Isaac.

At about five minutes to twelve, Hanna climbed into her car and headed toward Tisha's house. Her mind had waffled all morning. Should she go? Should she cancel? Should she go? Should she cancel?

In the end, she decided she needed to go. She had accepted an invitation. And by now, Tisha had probably put effort into making a lunch. So, as her parents had always taught her, follow through with your commitments. And she had committed to lunch. So she would follow through.

The drive just out of town was very pretty from the town limits. As soon as you exited the town proper, the scenery turned into farmlands, lush landscapes, and cows grazing.

It was nice. And it was pretty. She saw the road, according to Tisha's map, and she turned right onto that road. About a half mile down that road was the sign that said *Welcome to the Barkley's*. And she knew she'd found the right place.

She pulled into the tree-covered driveway. Foliage blocked the view of the house, but as soon as the trees cleared away, she saw a magnificent looking home. It was all brick and stone, two stories. The beautiful lanai on the front was welcoming. Four rocking chairs, set in twos with a table in between on one side of the lanai, and two with a table in between on the other.

There were floral arrangements on the tables, and the home was inviting, but it looked expensive. Once again, the thought that Tisha was way out of her league raced through her mind, and she got a little nervous before exiting her vehicle.

She strolled up the sidewalk from her car, trying not to look like a total newbie who'd never seen a beautiful home before, in case Tisha was watching out the window.

Before she got to the front door, it opened and Tisha stood, always with her back ramrod straight, and her shoulders pulled back. But the semblance of a smile on her red-painted lips was welcome.

"Thank you for coming out to the house, Hanna. Come on in, please."

Tisha stepped back, and Hanna entered a huge foyer area. Bright, light-colored walls, a round mahogany table sitting in the middle with a beautiful floral arrangement gracing the center.

That was one of the things she'd always wanted, a large enough foyer to have a floral arrangement in the middle greeting her guests as they walked in.

"Well, your home is beautiful, Tisha."

Tisha looked around as if she hadn't seen it in a while, and then nodded. "Thank you. I've worked very hard. My ex was never home. It was all on me. He would, of course, write the checks for anything that I wanted to have done, but he didn't really care about what I did. So this is all my design idea."

Hanna felt sorry for her. She seemed lonely.

"I have lunch set up on the back patio. If you'd like to join me."

Hanna followed Tisha through the foyer and to the left. They stepped into a beautiful kitchen. My gosh, there was even a brick fireplace in the kitchen. Hanna's eyes lovingly caressed the fireplace. It was a beautiful, big, open-arched fireplace. The logs that were sitting in the grate were never used, and of course, positioned perfectly.

The cabinets were a dark, rich mahogany. The granite countertops were light, with mahogany-colored swirls running through. Everything matched perfectly. There were light fixtures over the counter, which screamed money. It made her nervous for some reason.

There was a table sitting across from the counter that also had a beautiful chandelier hanging over it. And then she saw the glass door that led out onto a small sun porch.

Tisha opened the door and held her hand out for

Hanna to precede her. "I made a pitcher of lemonade. I hope you like lemonade."

Hanna smiled. "I do. Thank you so much."

"Please take a seat."

Tisha sat uncomfortably in her chair across from Hanna.

Hanna sat perched on the edge of her chair, not sure what to think of this whole lunch thing now that she was here. Tisha did not exude warmth. That was a fact.

"Well, thank you for inviting me over here, Tisha. I'm so happy to see your home, and it's really nice to be able to get to know you a little bit better."

Tisha smiled. "It's nice to get to know you a little bit better too, Hanna. My son, as I've said, loves your cinnamon rolls, and he speaks so highly of the bakery. So I thought the least I could do was come in and see it for myself and then invite you to lunch. So here we are."

She lifted the lid on a container, which held a variety of sandwiches. "I had these made up this morning for us at the deli. I have tuna, smoked chicken, smoked turkey, and roast beef. Please help yourself. I wasn't sure what you would like."

"Oh, thank you so much. I'll take a turkey."

Hanna reached in and pulled a turkey club sandwich out of the container. Tisha pulled one out for herself and then closed the lid.

She poured them each a glass of lemonade and then stared at Hanna. For her part, Hanna set her sandwich on her plate and waited to see what the protocol would be. She also wasn't sure what to say. If she should start to eat, was there going to be a prayer? She folded her hands in her lap.

Tisha nodded. "No, no, please, go ahead. I was waiting for you to take the first bite."

She swallowed. "Oh, I'm sorry." Hanna picked up her sandwich and gently bit into it. She was relieved when Tisha picked hers up and did the same. Weird.

Hanna nervously asked, "Are you from Blossom Springs?"

"Not really. I was born in New York. My parents moved to Tampa about thirty years ago. I followed them there because I hadn't selected a college yet and wasn't sure what I was going to do. My father is an investment manager. He started his business after moving to Tampa and still lives there today."

"Do you get to see him often?"

Tisha sniffed lightly and shifted in her seat. "Not that often. We don't always see eye to eye, and I like to avoid the arguments."

"I understand that."

Hanna focused on finishing her sandwich and drank her lemonade. Tisha stood abruptly. "Let me show you the flooring that I have here, to see if you'll like it."

She pushed in her chair and followed Tisha out of the sunroom and through the kitchen to a small pantry-type room off the kitchen. There were building supplies and things stacked neatly in various places. On the floor was a stack of flooring and it was beautiful dark hardwood with graining in it.

"This is the flooring I have. My son tells me there is enough here for an 8x10 room. I'm not sure if one of the rooms that you're fixing up is that size or smaller, but you are certainly welcome to have this if you'd like. Otherwise, I'll have my son pack it up and take it to the thrift store."

Hanna knelt down and touched the wood. The satiny

finish was soft to the touch and truly much nicer than she'd have ordered for her little house. The graining in it had light golden strands through it. She stood and brushed her hands on her thighs. Her cheeks were warm. She felt a little embarrassed, kind of like a charity case. But she smiled brightly and said, "I love it. It's beautiful."

"Perfect. I can have my son take it to your place today. You'll just need to give me your address. And then I have this table over here." She stepped over to a table that was sitting alongside the left wall. "This table was a kitchen table that we had in our house for years. My ex has proclaimed that he does not want it and to be perfectly honest with you, neither do I. You are welcome to it. It was very expensive. It's very sturdy, and it's in excellent condi-tion. But I'm just ready for a change."

Hanna looked at the pretty table. It was lighter wood than the flooring, but it was in perfect shape. A nice round table. The chairs matched it. It would look elegant in her little bungalow. And she didn't have a table. "So thank you. I'd love this. Are you sure I couldn't give you some-thing for it? You don't have to just hand me things."

"Nope. It's yours if you'd like it."

Hanna thanked her again. And then Tisha stood stock still.

Hanna wasn't sure what to do. She cocked her head to the side and looked Tisha in the eye.

"Is everything all right, Tisha?"

She saw Tisha's lip quiver slightly and then she inhaled a deep breath. "My ex-husband... who owns a business and whom I was married to the entire time he was building said business, has cut me off. I have no more alimony coming in and I am not sure that I'm really cut out for work. Not anything that I would be able to find in town here. And I'm not sure what to do."

Hanna's heart hurt for Tisha. She was out of her element. You could tell she had always had money, and she wasn't used to working. That was obvious from the manicured nails to the makeup to the expensive clothing that she wore.

"I can't believe if you've been married for a long time and your husband built a business the entire time that you were married, that you don't have some ownership in that business."

Tisha squared her shoulders back. "Yes, that's what I thought was weird, too. But my attorney did not feel as though I had any stake in the business because I never worked it."

Hanna cocked her head to the side. "I think you need a new attorney because I have a friend who went through the same thing, and from what I'm told, that because her staying at home and raising the children and keeping the house allowed the husband to go off to work and build that business, she was entitled to 10% of the profits for the rest of the life of the business. So I encourage you to find another attorney."

Tisha's head cocked, and she studied Hanna for a long time, almost to the point that Hanna felt a little uncomfortable. "Is that so? You know, Hanna, I think you're right. I don't think the attorney that I hired did me any justice. So I'm going to take your advice and I'm going to find another attorney. A female attorney. Thank you."

Hanna nodded, "You're welcome. We women have to stick together, don't we?"

"That we do."

Hanna concluded her lunch with the promise that

Tisha's son would be bringing the flooring and the table and a couple little pieces of pottery that Tisha said she no longer wanted over to Hanna's house tonight.

Hanna had a date though, so she was going to have to ask her neighbor, Tim, to let Tisha's son in to drop the things off. That should work out just fine.

Now she could look forward to her date.

But she still had an attorney meeting to get through, and that could prove to be trying.

Quinn had a pretty good outlook on life. Things managed to work out for him in the end. But sometimes that middle could be a rocky road. Today, for the first time, he felt as though he'd not only made it down the rockiest part of the road, but he'd turned the corner, and the horizon was beautiful.

He strode through the construction trailer at the Winston job site and chuckled when he saw nothing but crumbs left in the cinnamon roll box. Those guys devoured the box in less than five minutes. He had entered the construction trailer and within minutes, his guys practically stampeded the trailer to get one of Hanna's cinnamon rolls.

He picked up the empty box and tossed it in the garbage can. Then he pulled a paper towel from the corner holder and wiped up the crumbs, coffee drips, and frosting droppings. Tossing the paper towel in the garbage, he strode toward the door.

As he twisted the handle, his phone rang. He pulled it

from his pocket and saw Margo Price's name on the screen. He couldn't help how his heartbeat increased. She likely had news for him.

"Hello, Margo. How are you?"

She chuckled. "I'm feeling rather proud of myself, to be honest. Your offer has been accepted."

He chuckled and rocked back on his heels. "That's fantastic. Thank you so much for working your magic."

She laughed out loud. "Not sure how much magic there was. But to hear from them so soon tells me they are extremely motivated. Therefore, let's not miss our deadline. Will you be ready by Wednesday to close?"

"I'll be ready. I'll call my financial guy right after we hang up and make sure he has the ball rolling."

"Perfect. Congratulations, Quinn. I'll get you copies of the paperwork and the Army will have someone begin drafting the closing documents. As soon as I get them, we can close and exchange keys for funds."

His heart raced. He couldn't wait to tell Jared and Hanna. They'd celebrate tonight and have something fun to chat about. Which made him snap back to the present. "Can I grab those keys again to show someone the barracks?"

Margo chuckled. "Sure. I have some errands today, but just drop by the office and I'll have them up front for you."

"Thanks, Margo. I appreciate all you've done."

She laughed again. The sound filled him with promise and happiness. This was indeed a great day.

Quinn left the construction trailer and hopped into his truck. He couldn't wait to spread the news. He couldn't wait to start on the barracks. And he couldn't wait to develop the plan that Hanna had suggested in turning his barracks into housing for former military members who came to work for him.

As well as those who came to work for Sid and Jace. They'd have places for their new workers to go, and they'd be comfortable, and affordable for them until they got on their feet.

It would be perfect.

So many of these people suffered from things, including PTSD from their military lives. Now they'd have a comfortable place to live, and he would be there to help them deal with things. Maybe he'd even get a doctor to stop by and offer group therapy or some other types of therapies that would help them out.

This was his mission. He finally had a clear path. His mission was to help these men and women not only survive getting out of the service, but thrive. They'd have employment, housing, and therapy. It seemed perfect.

Oh, he couldn't wait to tell Hanna. As he started to drive toward home to change his clothes, his phone rang again.

He chuckled without even looking at who was calling. He tapped the button on his steering wheel.

"Hello, Quinn Kurtz."

Silence met him and then a clipped voice, one that sent a chill down his spine, responded. "Well, you certainly seem happy."

His ex-wife.

Buzzkill. With a capital B.

He didn't hide his exasperation. "What do you want now?"

She sniffed slightly. "Well, now I'm wondering what you were so happy about."

He shook his head. "It doesn't matter. What do you want?"

Silence again for a moment and he started to get irritated. She was quickly killing his buzz. That was a fact.

"Well, I wanted to let you know that I found a new attorney today and we are taking you back to court. I am entitled to a percentage of your business since I'm the one that allowed you the time and energy to build that business while I took care of everything else. The house, the bills, the kids, everything."

His neck stiffened, and his shoulders went back. "I'll have you know I took care of all the bills. Without me out there busting my ass, there would have been no money to pay for those bills."

"Nevertheless, I'm the one who took care of getting them paid. If you'll also remember, in the very beginning, I was the one who helped you send out your invoicing. So I was part of the business even though you like to ignore, or forget, that fact."

He was silent for a moment. He took a deep breath and let it out slowly.

"Do whatever you're going to do. I don't really care anymore. I'm finished paying you."

He tapped the phone button on his steering wheel to end the call. He took a deep breath and let it out slowly.

Swinging the truck around toward Margo Price's office, he cleared his throat and rotated his head. Moving his shoulders back and forth, he then decided he'd deal with this on a different day.

He'd go to Margo's and get his keys. That would get his happy mojo back. As he pulled into the parking lot, he let out a sigh, nodded his head, and sent up a silent prayer before he jumped out of his truck. He was not going to let her ruin this day for him.

He strode into Margo Price's real estate office and was greeted by a fresh face and a big smile. That was what he needed.

"Hi, Quinn. Are you here for the keys?" Becky, the receptionist asked.

"I am. Thank you so much."

"I've got them right here. Congratulations. This is going to be great for the town. Margo said you are going to make apartments out of the barracks. That's gonna look so much better down there. I can't wait to see what you do with it."

He chuckled. "Well, I hope I make you proud. I hope I make the entire town proud, to be honest with you."

She handed him the keys, a big smile on her face. Her fingernails were painted a light pink with some beachy scene on them. She always painted her nails and had some fun scene on them. It was something he'd always remembered about her, even as a younger girl. She'd graduated with his son, Jared, and if he recalled correctly, she was engaged to be married. A quick glance at her empty ring finger and he wasn't sure now. And he sure as hell wasn't going to ask either.

So he just nodded. "Thank you so much, Becky."

"You're welcome. How's Jared doing these days?"

Quinn smiled a genuine smile. Talking about his kids was always something he enjoyed. "Jared is doing great. He's working with me at Kurtz Construction and I'm going to make him the lead on the barracks project."

"Oh, wow. Isn't that nice? Good for him. He'll do a great job with it. He's a smart one."

Quinn nodded, his smile still in place. "He certainly is. Thank you for that."

Becky smiled, shrugged her right shoulder, and nodded. "Sure thing. Just telling it like it is."

He squeezed the keys in his hand and nodded.

"Oh, Margo said you don't need to bring those back. It's yours in a few days, anyway."

He nodded. "Thank you. Both of you." He nodded and stepped out of the door.

Yes, there was his mojo. It was back.

15

H anna sat next to her father at the conference table in Attorney Grant Park's office. The room was stifling. It wasn't that anything was bad here. The room was very clean, and pristine. The plethora of oak shelves were lined with law books. Some of them looked to be old and unused.

The paint on the walls was a light blue. The hanging pictures were what you'd expect to see in any attorney's office. George Washington, historical figures, a picture of Abraham Lincoln, and a picture of the Lincoln Law Library. But the last time she'd been in this office, she was getting divorced. And it made her feel like a failure. She felt like that again. She'd failed her sweet, nice, wonderful parents by bringing a dishonest, lying sack of crap to their doorstep. And she continued to bring that sad use of skin to their doorstep time and time again. It just made her feel sad. Her stomach twisted, and she slowly rested her hand against her belly to stop it from quelling.

She swallowed as Grant listened to her father's

recount of all the miserable things Isaac had done, and the things he was doing now. Again.

Every so often, Grant's eyes would float to hers and she saw the look of pity on his face. She hated his pity. She hated everyone's pity. He probably thought she was stupid and how in the world did these nice people end up with a daughter who was dumb as a rock? She'd put up with Isaac's bullshit so many times.

Sitting here now, listening to her father recount it all, she couldn't believe she'd tolerated so much. And now, the new crimes. Stealing money from her bank account. Catfishing women. How did one even think of all of this shit? Why did she ever, ever, ever let herself get in this position?

But Grant listened, and then he took a deep breath and addressed her. "Hanna, did these women give you any identifying information other than their names? Do you know how we can reach them?"

"No. One of them said she was going to work really hard to find an attorney who was going to find me at fault and then she'd be in touch." Hannah sighed, then sat up straighter. She pulled her phone from her little purse. "I have their numbers on my phone."

Grant nodded. She showed him the numbers, and he wrote them down. At least she could help that much.

Grant continued, "Well, what we can do right now is put together a plan of action. If anyone else calls you, have them call me immediately. Give them my name and my phone number. We'll get the information we need from them. We'll let them tell their stories, which, honestly, is really what they want. They want someone to talk to about this and, of course, they'd like their money back. But, mostly, they want someone to tell them Isaac is a terrible person and how did someone as smart as them get wrapped up with a loser like him? They want to know they aren't alone, and in these two cases, they are not. But so many others over time have been in similar situations. And they want to know they aren't stupid. He is just that good of a liar.

"Hopefully, they're the only two, but time will tell. I guess, as is often the case in these situations, these women start looking for each other and finding each other, and then they'll band together. But my office can make sure you're not bothered and you don't have to listen to any of them bad mouth you or ridicule you or threaten you. All you need to do is say, call my attorney. His name is Grant Park. Here's his phone number. Then hang up."

She swallowed the knot in her throat. "Okay." She tried really hard not to let her shoulders sink. Inhaling deeply, she picked her shoulders back up.

She was not to blame for this. She might be a little stupid, but she was not to blame for this. This was all Isaac's doing. And once again, he was trying to drag her down some deep dark hole, but she wasn't going to let him.

"Okay. Is there anything else?"

Her father nodded. "The bank is making her whole. However, as of this morning, it wasn't completed yet. I'm now on her account and will watch it daily. I also set up a text communication with the bank. Anytime money is spent from her account, I'll get a text and I can immediately deal with any of Isaac's scams."

Grant wrote this information down and shook his head. "This guy, huh? Hanna, I'm so glad you got away from him."

She nodded. "Me, too."

She was happy. What more could she say?

"Okay. I'll be in touch with the president of the bank too, to make sure that happens. Have they deposited some of the money?"

Her dad nodded. "They've made a couple of deposits, but not in full. Apparently, they are putting the money back into the account in the order it had been withdrawn as the bank is doing their forensic accounting. They just wanted to make sure her account had money in it for now."

"Okay. Well, keep your eye on that. They're also afraid you'll sue them for their employee's deception. After all, as a depository, they have a fiduciary duty to protect their customers' money. Make sure they make her whole and let me know if anything stalls on that front. I can contact the bank myself then. What about the business account?"

"He's never had access to that. They were divorced already when Hanna came home to run the bakery. I've always managed the bakery account and still am."

Grant nodded and stood. "Good. Thank you both for coming in. I'm sorry we're once again dealing with Isaac, but please don't worry. My office will have this all covered."

He reached out and shook her dad's hand. He then reached forward and shook her hand. He wrapped his left hand around hers and shook her hand with both of his. He looked her in the eyes. His were kindly blue eyes, with light creases around them from years of laughter and probably irritation from some of his clients and some of the things he had to do. But he smiled genuinely, and he said, "We've got this, Hanna. We're going to protect you. And you call if you need anything at all, or if you have any questions."

"Okay. Thank you, Grant. I really do appreciate it." She swallowed the knot that formed in her throat and took a deep breath to stem the flow of tears. "I appreciate your time on such short notice as well."

Grant nodded. "Anything for a couple of cinnamon rolls, I'll tell you that. My wife is hooked." He patted his stomach. "I guess I have to admit I am, too."

She chuckled, and it felt wonderful. She'd been tense the entire time they were here. Actually, she'd been tense for the past few days. It really was time to let somebody else handle some of this stuff.

She nodded her head. "Thank you. And please stop by. I've got a couple on the house for you for taking care of us so quickly."

Grant nodded. "I'm not going to turn that down. I'll be around later on today."

Her cheeks heated, and she smiled. "You do that."

He opened the door, and she stepped out first. Her father behind her.

The receptionist behind the desk, Ms. Jailisa Burns, was as professional as ever, an older lady who Hanna had known most of her life. "Thank you all for coming in."

Hanna smiled and waved. "Thank you, Ms. Burns. Nice seeing you."

Her father nodded to Jailisa, then rushed to the outside door to open it for her. Hanna stepped from the cool, serene air-conditioned law office to the sweltering heat of the Florida summer afternoon. It hit her like a brick. She moved along with her father to his car sitting at the curb. The law office was across the town square from her bakery, but her father wanted to drive. Likely due to the heat and humidity. She'd be drenched by the time she walked around the square, and she had a date tonight.

Her father opened the car door for her and said, "I told you he'd take care of everything for us."

Hanna nodded. "Yes, he's always been good to us, hasn't he, Daddy?"

"He sure has, sweetheart. We're not going to let Isaac do anything more to you. You made the hardest decision to leave him and divorcing him. That should have been the end of it, but we're going to make sure now it is."

She sat in the passenger seat, hooked her seat belt, and took a deep breath. After her dad had taken his seat, attached his seatbelt, and started the car, the air blowing from the vents was hot for a second, but cooled down quickly as he drove.

"Thank you so much, Dad. I'm so embarrassed. And feel like a fool. I feel so angry at all that Isaac has put me through. But I'm angrier at what he's put you and Mom through. I'm so sorry."

Her sweet father glanced briefly toward her, then back to the road. "You don't worry about a thing." He stopped at the stop sign and waited as a big blue pickup truck rumbled through. "Now, do you need to stop anywhere before we go back to the bakery?"

"No, thank you. I'm sure Mom needs a break right now and I have things to bake for tomorrow."

He chuckled. "Yes, she misses the bakery a lot, but she does like her naps in the afternoon."

Hanna smiled.

Her dad turned to the left and pulled up in front of the bakery. "Why don't you come on over for supper tonight? I'll grill us some steaks and we can sit and visit."

Her heartbeat sped up. She didn't want to lie to her parents about anything. Especially in light of all they were once again doing for her.

"I can't Dad. I have plans, and things to get ready for tomorrow. There's a fishing tournament in town and I have to bake additional buns and bread for the Sandbar. How about another night?"

"That sounds good, sweetheart."

Hanna glanced around the square at all the buildings. This had been home for so many years and while there was some comfort in being back, she kind of felt like a stranger once again.

So many new people here she didn't know, but she was going to remedy that. She was going to get to know people. She needed support around this town in case Isaac decided to come here.

And she had a date tonight. Time to get her head on straight and enjoy herself.

16

Quinn helped Hanna into his truck, happy he'd run it through the car wash in town and cleaned it up. He practically strutted around the front of the truck, his chest was puffed out slightly. His grin was so large he felt his cheeks tighten as he climbed inside.

Hanna chuckled. "You seem quite happy."

"I am happy. I have a date with a beautiful woman, and I found out today the Army has accepted my offer."

Hanna's smile lit up the truck. "Congratulations. That's wonderful." Her face turned to his. Those captivating blue eyes had him mesmerized. The adorable dimples in her cheeks begged for attention too. He stared into her eyes unabashedly as his heartbeat increased.

His smile grew. "Would you like to go see it?"

"Really? Yes. I'd love that."

He chuckled and pulled away from the curb in front of the bakery. His heart beat so quickly he struggled to breathe. She was intoxicating.

The town square was a one-way road forcing all vehicles to enter to the right and circle around. He drove by the courthouse, then rounded the corner and passed by the Law Office, Hair Salon, then his construction office. Jared's truck was parked in front. Jared was hauling flooring out of the front door. Quinn slowed but didn't honk or make any comment.

Hanna chuckled, "Isn't that Jared? Oh, that's your office, right?"

Quinn nodded. "Yep that's my office, and I don't know what Jared's doing with that flooring. I just ordered it for a big job across town."

Hanna shrugged. "Well, he's a good kid. I'm sure he's just helping out."

Quinn nodded. "He is a good kid. I'll touch base with him tomorrow. It's nothing to worry about tonight."

He continued around the square and turned right on Main Street. They had a great town here. He'd always loved that the businesses were kept up. And he enjoyed living here. It didn't hurt the weather was great, too, and frankly, it was home. As they drove past the Canning Vet Clinic, Shannon Canning was outside helping a pup into a car. He tapped the horn quickly and waved. Shannon waved in return.

He turned to Hanna. "Do you know Shannon Canning? She's quite a bit younger but her family owns the Canning Cattle Ranch out of town."

Hanna nodded. "Oh, well, I remember them from back in the day."

"Shannon's now a veterinarian and owns the vet clinic."

"Oh, that's so awesome."

"She's doing a wonderful job there, and she's still the vet at the ranch, too."

Hanna chuckled. "She's a busy girl. I think Mom and Dad told me she got married a while back."

Quinn chuckled, "Yeah they got married. Then they got divorced, and oddly enough they're getting married again."

"To each other?"

He chuckled, "Yep to each other."

Pulling into the parking area near the barracks, he glanced around and didn't see any vehicles. Relief filled his chest. Hopefully, the boarded-up window had deterred the partiers.

He pulled up to the main building. "So there's three buildings here on the property and I think I can make twelve apartments out of each building. Obviously, I'm only going to do them one at a time, and as I fill them, I'll go on to the next building. I'm going to build them so that they can be converted to condos if there's a demand, so veterans coming into town will have the opportunity to own a place rather than rent."

Hanna turned to face him. Her smile was beautiful. "I think that's wonderful."

"I know that Sid said he was only going to hire veterans at the garage as he needed them, and I know that's Jace's number one priority as well. So between us, and a few other businesses in town only hiring veterans, I think we'll be just fine. We can bring on other people, too, as long as they meet certain qualifications.

Hanna grinned. "What are those qualifications?"

Quinn chuckled, "Well I'm a businessman so they have to be able to pay their rent and they have to be employed unless they can prove to me that they have money some- where along the way to pay their rent, but otherwise I just want to keep it a nice place for people to live. I don't want any troublemakers. I don't want any drug dealers. I want only people who want to be here. It's not an easy feat sometimes."

Hanna nodded. "Oh, you've got that right. Those are good criteria."

"So this is the first building we're going to work on. It faces the street, so I think that's going to be the best idea for putting on a better face for these barracks, and once it's remodeled and looking appealing and inviting, I think that will draw even more attention to the place."

He opened his door and hopped out. Excitement once again coursed through him. He opened her door and the instant her hand lay in his; he felt the electricity sizzle up his arm. He stared into her eyes, eager to see if she felt the same as he did.

Her lips trembled slightly, and he saw her throat move as she swallowed. It felt amazing to be entering into a relationship with someone who felt the same way he did. He closed her door and took her hand in his. Her hand felt perfect in his. He enjoyed the feeling of this connection. It had been so fucking long since he'd felt a connection to anyone romantically.

He cleared his throat lightly. "So this first building is a bit of a mess. Kids or someone has been having parties inside and there's graffiti sprayed on the walls and even a pile of partially burned debris in the middle of the floor. We've boarded up a broken window, which hopefully will keep them out. But we'll be getting it all cleaned up soon."

She smiled sweetly. He reluctantly let go of her hand to unlock the door. The locks easily opened, and he pulled the door open wide. He felt inside and flipped on the lights, which flickered on slowly.

He then stepped back and waited for Hanna to enter ahead of him.

She wore a cute little white denim skirt and a pretty blue top that matched her eyes.

He continued his explanation. "So as you can see, this is a three-story building." He motioned between two rooms. "I think I can take these two rooms and part of this third one and make it a nice bedroom with its own bathroom. Kitchen, living room, bedroom, so one bedroom is here and then upstairs. I think I can have fewer apartments, but make them two bedrooms so it would use three different barracks rooms to make two bedrooms. They'll be small, almost tiny house small, but they'll be efficient and safe and everything will be brand new."

Hanna laughed. "You seem so excited about this. I'm really happy for you, Quinn. I'm very excited about what you'll do here."

He turned to face her. He stared into her eyes. "Thank you again for the suggestion to make it veteran housing. I love the idea and hopefully, they won't have too much of a qualm about coming to live in an old barracks. Sometimes the barracks living experiences weren't the best."

Hanna smiled at him. They stood face to face, her long dark hair hung down in waves. The urge to kiss her was so strong he nearly lost his breath.

He leaned forward slowly, watching her eyes as he neared. His breath quickened. His lips touched hers, softly. He pressed his lips firmer to hers, wanting to feel her lips completely. His lips moved against hers, and she matched his movements. A thrill ran up his spine as he stepped closer and wrapped his arms around her body. She felt wonderful against his chest. Her arms wrapped around his waist and her hands slid up his back, holding him to her. Head rush - he got a head rush. She felt so good.

He pulled back slightly, laying his forehead on hers. Both of them dragged in breaths as they stood together.

He whispered, "I've wanted to do that for a while now."

She dragged in a breath. "I've wanted you to do that."

He kissed her forehead softly. More to allow him time to catch his breath and gather his equilibrium than anything else. Her stomach growled, and he pulled back.

"I'm not being a very good date. I promised you dinner and we're kicking around in this old dirty building while your tummy is protesting."

She chuckled. "I had a busy day and didn't really eat much. But I'm honored that you were willing to show me your new project."

"Thank you for coming to see it. I hope you'll be pleasantly surprised when you see the finished product."

"I can't imagine I won't be."

He turned toward the door, taking her hand once again in his. Flipping off the light switch, he locked the door with one hand, pulled it tightly closed, and led his beautiful companion to the truck to start their date in earnest.

As he pulled into the parking lot at the Sandbar, he saw his guys working on the stage in the back.

Hanna grinned. "Are those your guys up there?"

He chuckled, "Yep they sure are hard workers. It's seven o'clock at night and here they are still putting in a long day."

"That's really nice. You're fortunate to find people like that."

"That I am."

They exited the truck, and he took her hand as they

navigated the beach area toward the back of the Sandbar. He waved as one of the guys stopped and looked at him. He waved in return and turned them toward the hostess podium near the back door. "There are two of us, and we'd like to sit out on the beach if possible."

"Oh, sure Quinn." She checked her chart. "Let's see..." She frowned slightly. "I'm sorry to tell you this, but all I have available right now is in front of the stage. I'm guessing that there'll be a day when that is a very popular seat, but right now, with the construction going on, it's not so popular."

Quinn chuckled and glanced at Hanna. Her smile and nod were all he needed. "Since it's my guys up there, I'm happy to sit in front of the stage.

Hanna chuckled. "I could watch people work all day."

They both laughed. His spirits were so high his heart hammered in his chest. My goodness, she was a catch.

17

anna sat as Quinn pulled out her chair. He helped her scoot her chair in since it wasn't that easy on the sand. But the weather was warm and beautiful. The water lapping on the shore of the beach was serene music.

And she was sitting across the table from the most handsome man she had seen in...what was it? Forever.

He was handsome.

His dark hair and beautiful dark eyes made it difficult for her to look away.

His skin was tanned from being out in the sun, which she knew wasn't necessarily healthy for a person. But he sure wore it well.

And when he kissed her, man, her knees shook. She hadn't been kissed like that in... well, that was also forever.

Isaac wasn't much of a kisser. His pinched little lips pecking at her all the time, not wanting to really melt their lips together. That should have been a sign to her that he wasn't necessarily into her as much as he was into looking for a sugar mama to take care of everything he needed.

And she was just that idiot, too.

There were so many periods of time when he didn't work. And she was out working every day trying to make a living to pay their bills.

Here, all this time, he was just looking for a way to scam other people.

She fisted her hands together and released them when Quinn leaned forward. She shouldn't be thinking about Isaac right now. She had a wonderful man sitting across from her. At least she hoped he was a wonderful man. But she was willing to give him a chance. After all, nobody could be worse than Isaac.

Quinn grinned. "You look like you're a million miles away."

She blinked and let out a breath. "I'm sorry. I just kind of had a miserable day. But it's better now."

He cocked his head to the side. His full lips turned down at the corners slightly. "Do you want to talk about it?"

She smiled. "No. No, not only do I not want to talk about it, but I want to stop thinking about it. Just some things kind of hang on for a while."

He nodded. "Oh, I know exactly what you mean. My day was full of mixed emotions, too. Happy, sad, happy, sad."

She cocked her head to the side. "Do you want to talk about it?"

He leaned back and laughed. "No. No, I don't. But in all fairness of sharing and all. My ex is taking me back to court for more money."

Her lips stretched down into a frown. "I'm sorry."

He reached over and took her hand in his. "I'm sitting here with a beautiful woman and I want us to get to know each other and not talk about our terrible days. I only said anything at all, because I wanted you to know that my life isn't perfect either."

She nodded. "I'm sorry for that, but...Deal."

He squeezed her fingers. "How do you feel being back in Blossom Springs?"

She smiled. "It's weird. It's like being home again and then it isn't. So many things have changed. Even the drive down Main Street showed new stores and, well, for instance, Shannon Canning's Vet Clinic. That wasn't here the last time I was back here. So as much as it's home, it's a different home."

He nodded. "Yup. That's what happens when you leave for a while and then come back. Your memories are of the way things used to be and yet people don't respect that and go ahead and make changes."

She laughed. "I guess you're right there. I didn't think about it."

"When was the last time that you were back here?" He asked.

She shrugged. "Oh, I guess it was about six or seven years ago. I came home for my parents' anniversary. But normally, Mom and Dad would come out by me and we would meet once a year somewhere else for vacation. Mom likes to go to other places, and it had always been kind of a tradition of ours to have a week's vacation some-where away from both of our businesses and all of our worries and woes.

"So I would meet Mom and Dad and we would go wherever Mom had picked for the year. And we've been to many places. We've tried the mountains, we've been to different beaches, and we've been in condos in the downtown area of large cities. And then we've been in little, tiny houses off the beaten path where we didn't really have much of anything to do but sit around and chat. They've all been nice. They've all been comforting. I love spending time with my parents."

Quinn nodded. "That sounds wonderful, actually. I'm glad you have a close relationship with them."

She sighed. "How about you? Are you close to your parents?"

He licked his lips, and she watched him process his thoughts. His eyes were so expressive. "Well, my parents are both gone. Dad died about ten years ago. He had cancer. And Mom died about six years ago. To be honest with you, I think she just kind of had a broken heart. But the official cause of death was a heart attack."

Hanna squeezed his fingers. "I'm sorry. That's never easy. And I dread the day when I have to live through it myself."

Quinn nodded. "Yes, it's not easy, even if you had the chance to prepare yourself. It's still a finality. But you still have your parents. All I can say, if I have to give some advice, is enjoy them while they're here. There are no guarantees for tomorrow."

She nodded. "You're right. You're absolutely right. And so what is on the horizon for Quinn Kurtz besides repurposing an Army barracks?"

He laughed and leaned back. And she enjoyed watching him, but she missed holding hands with him. His broad shoulders fit his shirt nicely. He wore a button-up short-sleeve dress shirt. And he had khaki pants on.

She remembered how he looked so casual when he walked into the bakery and yet professional. And handsome. But she had the feeling that Quinn was always thinking about what he was going to do next. That was kind of a detriment to most businesspeople. It was hard to get away from it because so much responsibility was required to run a business.

"Well, I'm with this Army barracks project. I'm going to get Jared involved in general contracting, so in a few years, I can start taking some more time off. He's smart. He'll catch on quickly. He can do it. But mostly, I think he's ready. So that's what's on the horizon for Quinn Kurtz and Kurtz Construction."

Hanna nodded. "You know, that sounds pretty good. Nice job planning ahead."

He laughed. "I can't tell you that I've always had the knack to plan ahead this far. But I'm really happy that I'm doing it now."

The waitress came and took their drink and their meal order. They sat quietly, making idle chitchat. But mostly, what was on Hanna's mind was she hoped he kissed her again tonight. She was really looking forward to that.

She leaned back in her chair just as the construction workers jumped off the stage and walked toward them.

Quinn sat up straight. Ever the businessman. "Hey guys, nice work. How are you doing?"

They nodded. "We're doing alright. We just wanted to let you know we should be able to finish up in two days. All the supplies came in. And we're going to work long days tomorrow and the next to get this project finished for Jace."

Quinn smiled. "Thank you so much. We both appreciate that." His eyes met hers. "Have you two met Hanna Valentine?"

The younger of the two men looked her in the eyes and grinned. "She's the cinnamon roll lady."

Hanna laughed, her cheeks heated. She had the feeling this was going to be her new nickname.

"That I am."

He nodded. "I think the entire town knows who the cinnamon roll lady is."

Quinn chuckled and winked at her. "Well, Hanna, you've got a nickname. I hope you love it."

She laughed. "It's good marketing."

"Anyway," he said, "I want to introduce you to Brian and Sam. Both of these guys just started with me about three or four months ago. And they've been fine, fine workers. I'm very happy to have them on board. Brian served in the Army. Sam is a Marine. Both served honorably and I couldn't be prouder to have them on staff."

Both men's cheeks were tinted pink. And she had noticed that always seemed to be the norm with former military. While they were proud of their service, they sometimes were a little embarrassed to have that service acknowledged.

She leaned forward, held her hand out, and shook their hand. "Thank you for your service." She said to both of them.

They both nodded, their eyes sliding towards Quinn's every now and then. She thought it was cute.

And she could tell the respect they had for Quinn, which she thought was a testament to what kind of man he was.

Life was looking up!

18

Quinn drove Hanna back to the bakery. He got out of the truck and walked her to the back door.

She unlocked it and let them both in. "Can I make you some coffee? Cinnamon roll? I have a couple left in the bakery case."

He chuckled and patted his tummy. "I think I've had enough to eat. As delicious as they are, I don't think I could eat a cinnamon roll. I wouldn't mind a cup of coffee though if you're serious."

She chuckled. "I'm absolutely serious. Let me go out front and get it."

He followed her out to the front of the bakery and watched as she deftly made another pot of coffee.

"How many of those do you make a day?"

She laughed. "I don't know. Some days fifteen, some days twenty, I don't know. I lose count."

"You sure do look like it's done by memory. It looks effortless."

She laughed. "Yep, that would be from days and days and weeks of making pots of coffee."

She set the empty coffee pot under the burner, turned the coffee maker on, and then turned to face him. They stared at each other for a long time.

Quinn's heartbeat was erratic. His lips remembered the feel of her lips from earlier and his body responded to her in different ways. He stepped toward her and was pleased to see that she took steps toward him as well. The instant they stood in front of each other he reached forward, wrapped his arms around her, and looked into her eyes.

He whispered, "Hanna you are the most beautiful woman I've ever seen."

He heard her exhale and took the opportunity to touch his lips to hers once again. This time, their kiss was more urgent. Their lips moved in unison with each other. His tongue swiped along her lips, and she opened her mouth to let him in. That was just about the undoing of him. He deepened their kiss. His right-hand dove into the back of her hair. It was soft and silky. She smelled fantastic. Like citrus and baked goods and all things wonderful, and she felt even better. Her arms wrapped around his waist. Her hands slid up his back as they had done earlier, and this time she pulled him closer to her. Their kisses became urgent. His body was on fire. His cock roared to life, and he wasn't sure where to go from here. He knew where he wanted to go but they were in a bakery. There wasn't a bed to be seen, and he didn't know where she lived. She'd kept that kind of quiet.

He slowly kissed down the side of her neck. The soft little moan that she emitted urged him on further. His left hand slid between them and he gently squeezed her breasts. They were firm and heavy, and he'd never felt anything that felt so good in his life. That was the truth.

A moan escaped her throat once more, and he had to swallow a lump in his. He whispered near her ear, "My God, Hanna I want you so bad."

She pulled back slightly and stared into his eyes. They stood motionless for a moment, and he wasn't sure what her thoughts were. He was slightly worried he'd ruined the moment.

Instead, she grabbed his hand and walked them toward the back door. Just before they reached it, she turned to the right and there was a wooden door he hadn't noticed before. She really did spin his head around.

She opened the door but said quietly, "I stay here sometimes when I've been working really late. My place is, well it's a mess. I've been remodeling it as you know, and sometimes I just don't have the energy to go and fight through water issues or trip over construction materials, so I stay here. It's just a small little apartment up here, and when I get my place finished, I'll actually start working on the upstairs here to rent it out. But for right now, I'd love for us to enjoy it together."

Well, if that didn't spin his head out of control. He opened his mouth to say something, didn't know what he was going to say, closed it, and opened it again. "I'd love to share it with you."

And with that, he followed Hanna as if she were a siren singing his song up the stairs and into the small little apartment that was not much bigger than a matchbox. There was a small, tiny little kitchen with three cabinets. A very small refrigerator to the left.

Across the room was a small sofa and to the right of that was a bed. It was a small double bed, but for what they planned on doing, they'd only need that small double bed. He began unbuttoning his shirt with his free hand. He couldn't help but notice that his fingers shook slightly. It had been a while. Hanna stopped them at the foot of the bed and turned to face him.

She looked uncertain, and he saw her swallow. He put two fingers under her chin and lifted her head so that her eyes met his. "If you're having second thoughts, don't worry. I won't be mad. This will only work if we're both ready for it."

She smiled. "I'm ready for it. It's just..." She swallowed again. Her hands lifted out to the side and then dropped down. "It's just that it's been a while and well...it's just been a while."

He chuckled. "I was just thinking the same thing for myself. This would be my cue," he swallowed, "to ask about protection."

She chuckled. "Man, I'm so out of practice I didn't even think of that."

He grinned in return. "I understand it's what all the kids say these days." They both had a nice laugh and then she shook her head. "I haven't been with anyone for a long time, Quinn. By a long time, I'm saying more than two years. I'm clean."

He swallowed. His thoughts from earlier came running right back to him. She was a catch. "I'm clean too, Hanna. It's been a long time for me as well. Not quite two years, but long. More than a year."

She nodded. "Well, then I guess there's no need to worry about protection."

His lips clamped down on hers. This time all hesitancy was gone. Their lips barely left each other's as they divested themselves of their clothing. Once they were naked, he pulled back to look at her. She was beautiful. Full, firm breasts, her tummy was slightly soft, but still sexy as could be. He touched her breasts. Her skin was heated and soft and wonderful under his hands. He moved his thumbs over her nipples and enjoyed watching her lips slightly part.

"You're simply beautiful," he whispered.

Her eyes stared into his. She lifted her right hand and lay it on his chest. Her fingers moved through the hair on his chest, and over his nipple, causing it to pucker tightly. She leaned in and sucked his nipple into her warm, wet mouth and his cock roared to life. His hands wrapped around her body, enjoying the skin-to-skin contact. She stepped closer to him, her tongue blazing a wet trail around his nipple and up his chest. She stopped to kiss him there, then wrapped her arms around his waist.

"You feel so good against me," she whispered.

His voice was gruff when he responded. "You feel even better."

She chuckled against his chest, and he stepped away to lay her on the bed. She pulled the covers back and slid onto the bed and his eyes couldn't have looked away if the place had been on fire.

He slid in next to her, their bodies naturally turning toward the other, their lips once again mating. He rolled on top of her, holding himself up on his elbows. His lips found hers once more. Her legs rose up and wrapped around his waist, and his cock throbbed. He didn't want to rush this moment, but he wanted to be inside her so badly his brain nearly stopped working.

He reached down and positioned his cock at her entrance, and she moaned. God, he loved that sound.

His lips found hers as he slowly pushed himself inside

her wetness. She felt like heaven. Warm, tight, wet. Absolutely amazing. He reluctantly pulled out and pushed back in, and that feeling washed over him once more. His heartbeat increased, his skin heated and the feel of her hands exploring his body as he entered her again and again was like nothing he'd ever felt before. How had he never felt like this before?

He increased his pace, and she met his movements. They continued this dance, over and over, their bodies each striving for that oh-so-perfect ending, but he was determined to enjoy the journey.

He increased his pace again, and Hanna began to breathe heavily. "Quinn." She whispered. "Quinn."

He wanted her to always whisper his name as she came. He added pressure each time he pushed into her, his pace quickening to help her reach her climax. She called out his name once more before her body stiffened as she fell over the edge. He waited for her to enjoy the feeling, then began once again to achieve his own climax. She urged him on with her legs and her hands on his ass, until his balls pulled up tightly, painfully needing release. In that moment, the white-hot pain and pleasure surged through him as he let himself go.

Once his climax had finished, he rested on his elbows, his forehead pressed to Hanna's and his breathing rapid. Her hands massaged his back and her legs fell to the bed in spent relaxation.

She whispered, "That was fantastic."

He couldn't form words yet.

19

H anna dozed with her arms wrapped around Quinn. Well, at least her right arm. Her other arm was at her side. Her head lay on his arm.

He was breathing evenly and deeply. She lay with her eyes closed, listening to the soft even sound.

She just had sex with Quinn Kurtz. Their relationship just stepped up to the next level. She wasn't sorry.

But guilt gnawed at her. She needed to be upfront with him about Isaac and what was going on in her life. If they were to continue this relationship, he needed to know. Because knowing Isaac as well as she did, he would try in some way to blackmail Quinn or harm him.

She knew that to be a fact. And she wanted Quinn to know to protect his children in case Isaac tried to do something there, too. Hell, she hadn't even heard of catfishing people until this whole new thing cropped up. And she didn't know what else she didn't know.

Quinn's voice was growly, and heavily sleep-laden, when he said, "What are you thinking about?"

She mumbled, "How do you know I'm thinking?"

He chuckled. She felt it run through his lungs from deep inside. She liked the feeling of it as her arm lay across his chest.

"You ceased to be malleable. Your body started to stiffen. You're thinking."

She let out a breath and sat up. "With her right hand, she scraped her hair off of her forehead, shaking it out as she pulled it back. She turned her head to see Quinn watching her. His hand reached up and touched her curls.

"You have beautiful hair, Hanna. Actually, everything you have is beautiful."

She smiled. Her cheeks heated slightly. Good thing the room was still a little dark. Nothing illuminated it but the moon shining in the window.

"You're beautiful yourself, Quinn."

He chuckled. "I've never been called beautiful."

"Well, now you have."

His hands smoothed down her back. "What were you thinking about?"

She swallowed and twisted slightly in the bed to face him. "I think I need to tell you what's been going on in my life. If we're, I mean, I don't want to assume, but we, well, you know," her hand moved back and forth between them. "I mean, are we in a relationship? I mean, I don't do one-night stands. Kind of late for me to tell you that now. But are we, I mean, I don't want to assume, but do we..."

He laughed. And it was beautiful and melodic. And she could have listened to his laugh all day.

"If you're worried about whether or not I only wanted you for a one-night stand, please put your mind to rest. I want so much more than one night with you, Hanna. As far as are we in a relationship? Do you want to be in a relationship with me?"

She stared into his dark eyes for a while. The realization that she could stare into them for a long time crept forward in her mind.

She licked her lips. "Yeah, I do."

His smile widened. "Good. I do, too."

She nodded her head. "Then I need to tell you about some things going on in my life. Because I think you need to protect yourself."

He leaned up on his elbows and looked at her. "Protect myself from who or what?"

She swallowed again, dread filling her chest as she knew that she had to talk about her ex. What an icky subject to have after such a beautiful moment they'd just shared.

"My ex is a, well, let me say this, he's a criminal. He does criminal things. The trouble is he's not really gotten caught. And, actually, I didn't even know he was a criminal until recently."

And then she told him about all the things that had been going on and all the things that Isaac had done over the years. She saw his face turn to stone, his jaw clenched, and she could tell he didn't like Isaac any more than she did right now.

And she thought that was saying a lot because she didn't like Isaac at all anymore.

"Hanna, I'm so sorry that you've had to deal with anything like that. No one, especially someone as beautiful as you, should have to do that. But I'm glad you told me. And don't worry, that fucker isn't going to hurt me in any way. Or my kids."

She nodded, swallowed that giant lump that had grown in her throat, inhaled deeply, and then let it out in a whoosh.

"If you... if this changes your mind in any way, I understand." She softly said.

He sat up, slid his hands under her arms, and pulled her tightly to him as he laid back down. She lay on top of him, staring down into his beautiful face. She would call him beautiful all the time. Because he was. He was so handsome. And right now, his understanding meant so much to her.

He smoothed the hair back from her face, holding it softly back.

He kissed her lips, softly at first. His tongue swept out and slid across her bottom lip. She opened her mouth, wanting his tongue inside of her mouth.

She loved the way he kissed. His lips were full and soft and sensual. They covered hers and they made her feel like he truly, truly wanted to kiss her. It almost brought her to tears to think about how many times she had wanted this in her life and had to wait till she was forty-five years old to get it. I guess life happened in its own good time.

After they'd kissed for a while, she lifted her head. She looked down into his eyes.

He grinned slightly. "Something that someone else has done to you isn't going to make me change my mind. It's not as if you've done that. You are not a criminal. You've done nothing wrong. He has. Your only fault, if anything, is caring too much and not wanting to give up soon enough. And that's admirable. And I'm sure there's many times that you'd wished that you'd given up a lot sooner. But you have to admit that somebody who's willing to continually put themselves out there in the face of what you've had to endure over and over again says an awful lot about what kind of person you are. And that's a good quality person, Hanna. I'd never fault you for something someone else did. And anybody that would, isn't worth a salt."

She felt tears well up into her eyes and one dropped down onto Quinn's cheek before she could stop it.

His thumb swiped under her eyes softly to stop her tears from flowing.

"Please tell me that's the last tear you'll ever shed over that son of a bitch."

She smiled softly. "I'm not shedding a tear over him at all. I'm shedding a tear at what a beautiful man you are. So understanding. And I can't tell you how relieved I am to get this off my chest because I hated hiding it from you. I felt like a fraud. And I don't want to feel like a fraud with you, Quinn."

He kissed her a few more times. Rolled her over. And inserted himself into her.

The moan that escaped her throat as he did was his new favorite sound. His lips kissed her forehead. And her temples. As he slowly slid in and out of her, his heart swelled.

Her hands slid down his back and to his ass and squeezed. He liked that. His ass tightened as he pushed into her and her fingers tightened on his skin. He lifted slightly to look into her eyes, and he wasn't disappointed. She stared at him, her lips slightly parted and glossy from his kisses.

"You're sexy, Hanna."

Her lips lifted at the corners slightly.

His skin heated as he worked to bring her pleasure. He

wanted to watch her as she came. Adding pressure each time he fully entered her, he heard that moan, and each time it grew louder. He pushed in fully and her lips opened and she called out his name. "Quinn."

Then she tumbled over the edge of pleasure and he hurried to meet her there.

Wednesday morning Quinn hurried into Margo Price's office to sign the papers. As he signed his last signature to the final paper, which looked to be the size of a small mountain, he grinned.

Margo clapped her hands once. "Congratulations, Quinn."

She reached across the table to shake his hand, and his smile grew.

"Thank you. Now, I'm off to work."

Margo laughed. "I can't wait to see what you do with the place."

He sauntered out of the office, a folder full of copies of his signed paperwork tucked under his arm, a huge smile on his face, and excitement coursing through him.

He pulled out his phone and texted Hanna. "It's mine."

"Congratulations. Want to celebrate tonight?"

"I sure do. I'll call you later."

He drove to his office just as Jared arrived.

"Hey there. Let's have a little chat."

"Okay."

Jared followed him into his office with a fresh cinnamon roll and a cup of coffee in his hands. Quinn grinned as he watched his son devour the cinnamon roll. "There will come a day when you won't be able to devour those cinnamon rolls like you do now."

Jared chewed a bit, then mumbled with a mouthful of food. "I sure hope not."

Quinn chuckled. "Anyway, I signed the papers this morning and the barracks are mine. I'd like you to take the lead on this project."

"Really? That's awesome, Dad."

"I think you're ready, and I want to give you the opportunity. Besides, you'll need to work those cinnamon rolls off."

Jared laughed, took a drink from his coffee cup, and shrugged. "Jealous."

"Maybe." Quinn chuckled. "Anyway, take a crew to the barracks and begin with cleaning up the place. I've ordered the dumpsters to be delivered this morning. Leave Sam and Brian to finish the stage at Jace's. They can join you once that's finished. I have an interview with a potential new hire later this morning. Anyway, begin the demo after cleanup. We're starting with building one, and I'll be around with the architect later this morning to go over all of his plans with you."

Jared chuckled. "Seems as though you're pretty excited about this."

"I'm very excited."

Jared finished his cinnamon roll, then drank the rest of his coffee. He stood up, "Okay. Well, I won't let you down."

"I'm sure you won't. By the way, what were you doing the other night with the flooring you were hauling out of here?"

"That's the flooring for the job at Mom's. Remember, she's redoing the flooring in her sunroom."

Quinn nodded. "Don't order any more products for her without talking to me. She's beginning to take advantage. And I'm being generous with *beginning*."

Jared nodded. "I get it, Dad."

Jared left his office, and Quinn sat at his desk. The folder with his new paperwork lay in front of him. He unlocked, and pulled out his bottom file drawer, tucked the paperwork into his personal folder, and closed and locked his drawer.

He wiggled the mouse for his computer and brought it to life, then quickly opened his project management software. He changed the access to allow Jared to make changes in the barracks job then sat back and let his thoughts run back to Hanna.

They'd spent every day for the past week together in the evenings, having dinner together, getting to know each other, and making love. Best week of his life. But always at the apartment above the bakery.

He pulled his phone from his pocket and sent her a text.

"How about we have a picnic dinner on the beach tonight?"

She didn't respond right away and assumed she was probably busy, so he wasn't going to worry about it. She had a business to run as well.

He pushed back from his desk, eager to meet the architect at the barracks. Just as he was about to leave his office, a man walked in the front door with a folder in his hand.

His tone was clipped and businesslike. "Are you Quinn Kurtz?"

Quinn nodded. "Yes, I am."

The man pulled some papers out of the folder and held them in front of Quinn. "You've been served."

Quinn numbly took the papers from the man just before he turned and stalked out of the office. Quinn looked down at the papers in his hand. He was being taken to court by his ex.

Didn't that just figure? He read through the paper-work. It was just as she had told him. She was taking him to court to receive a portion of his business. The ask was twenty percent. He damn near choked on his spit. No way in hell he was going to give her twenty percent of his profits for doing absolutely nothing.

So rather than heading to the job site, he was now going to his attorney's office to drop off these new papers. He told himself, it didn't matter. Grant was a great attorney.

He walked down the street instead of hopping in his truck, because he needed to work off this irritation. That bitch followed through on her threats this time.

Grant was on the opposite end of the square as Quinn's office. The walk would do him good. He himself had been imbibing in a few extra cinnamon rolls this past couple of weeks. But that was the good part of his life right now and he wasn't sorry.

He walked into Grant's office, and Jailisa, Grant's receptionist, greeted him with a smile. "Morning, Mr. Kurtz. How are you?"

He nodded. "I'm fine, Jailisa. How are you? How's your boy?"

"Oh, he's doing very well. He's in college now you know."

"College? My goodness I didn't realize he was that old already."

She raised her hand up in the air. "Tell me about it. I can't believe he's in college either."

Quinn nodded. "Good luck to him. I'm sure he'll do fine. He's a smart boy."

"Thank you, Mr. Kurtz. How can I help you?"

"Is Grant in? I know I don't have an appointment, but I just received some papers. I've been served."

Jailisa nodded slowly. "I'll see if he's available. Hang on."

She pushed herself out of her chair and walked down the hall to Grant's office. Within a couple of minutes, Grant followed Jailisa down the hall toward him. "Hey, Quinn."

Grant reached forward and shook his hand. "I understand problems are afoot."

Grant motioned toward the conference room, and Quinn followed. "Yeah, it appears the ex wants twenty percent of my business for writing out a couple of bills back in the early days."

Grant scoffed. "Well, let's see what she's saying."

He sat quietly as Grant read through the motion. He hummed a couple of times and Quinn tried not to squirm.

"Well, let me first ask you this," Grant said. "Are you willing to offer her anything? And before you say no, let me advise you that she does have certain rights under the law. She didn't work while you were married. She did stay home and raise the kids. And she helped out with things around the house and took care of the home. In the courts' eyes, that's going to mean something. So they're going to be inclined to offer her something. As painful as it is for you to offer her anything, please know that I'm going to encourage you to offer her something. And it can be small, but at least it looks like you're willing to work with her. And for another thing, you're going to have to give it up, anyway. So how long do you want to drag this out? How much of a fight do you have in you? Because that's what I'm asking you now. And it does appear that she's willing to fight."

Quinn leaned back and huffed out a breath. He should have known it was too good to be true.

"Is five percent too much or too little?"

Grant shrugged. "Here's what I think we'll respond with. I need financials from you from the beginning of the business until the day of your divorce. She isn't entitled to anything from the business from the date of divorce until today. That's all after the fact. And I can't believe her attorney didn't fight for this for her in the divorce."

Quinn took in a deep breath. "If you'll remember, that's where the alimony payment amount came from. That's why it was so high. It was partially alimony and partially a settlement from the profits of the business at that time paid over five years."

Grant nodded. "Yes, I recall that now. I'll pull those papers and the Divorce Order and reacquaint myself with the terms and conditions. In the meantime, don't engage in conversation about this with her. Every communication about this goes through my office."

Quinn nodded, "Got it."

"And also, I understand you're working on the barracks. May I suggest that we create a separate LLC for that and put it in a separate account so it's not under Quinn Kurtz Construction, but as the owner and landlord it'll be under a whole separate entity? That's just protection moving forward, and we'll do the same with any other properties you purchase in the future."

"I just signed papers on that today."

"Yes, and she isn't in any way entitled to that property, but let's keep it nice and clean, okay?"

Quinn nodded. "Okay we'll go ahead and set up a new LLC for that. I can bring the closing paperwork down here in a few minutes, so you have the information on that and the copy of the deed to put that in the LLC's name."

Grant nodded, "Perfect. I'll get that straightened up. I'll look over this paperwork more completely, pull out the Divorce Order, and work up a response to this. I'll let you know when that's available to take a look at."

Quinn nodded. "Okay, thank you. Just give me a call when I need to come in and look at anything."

Grant nodded his head. Made a couple of notes on his tablet and Quinn settled in to resigning himself to the fact that his life wasn't perfect either. He'd tell Hanna tonight, so she'd feel a bit better about the shit going on in her life. They'd have a drink and laugh about it all, and then he'd make love to her again. It sounded like the perfect evening.

He shook hands with Grant and walked out the door. His phone chimed that he had a text. Glancing at his phone briefly as he strode toward his office, he saw Hanna's name and his spirits immediately soared.

"Congratulations! balloon emoji happy face emoji. I'm proud of you," she said.

His heart beat a little faster just seeing her name on his text. His heart swelled seeing that she was proud of him. He responded back with the lips emoji as a kiss, and said, "See you later."

Pocketing his phone, he got in his truck and headed toward his architect's office. Things could be worse. He was making great money. He was going to do just fine with this new venture, and he had a new girl in his life that he was so darned excited about.

21

H anna smiled as she bagged up the buns for the Sandbar, eager to drop them off. She was making money with the bakery and her account with the Sandbar helped immensely. She was happy with the direction her life was going. She really liked Quinn. He was, well, he was everything she'd always hoped for in a relationship. He was a gentleman. He was honest. He ran a good business, which meant he was gainfully employed. Something that Isaac never was. Well, unless you call scamming people gainful employment. She didn't.

Carrying the racks out to her SUV, she stacked them up inside, made sure the front door to the bakery was locked, grabbed her purse off the hook in the kitchen, and set out to deliver her buns. Her phone rang as she drove to the Sandbar, and she tapped the button on her steering wheel. "This is Hanna Valentine."

"Well, Hanna Valentine, I am so happy to speak with you. You owe me money, and I understand you've spoken to a couple of my friends this week, and you owe them money as well. And I just wanted you to know that we are working very hard to get an attorney to force you to pay us the money you owe us."

Hanna's heart beat quickly, and her stomach rolled. Another one. Another one. "My attorney's name is Grant Park. His phone number is 800-555-2121. Feel free to give him a call. That is all I need to tell you. Thank you."

She tapped the end call button. Her finger shook slightly, and she swallowed several times to dispel the icky feeling in her throat. How many more would there be? "Isaac, you truly are a piece of shit," she said out loud. She turned her SUV into the Sandbar parking lot and parked as close to the kitchen door as she could. She opened up the back of her SUV and began carrying the buns into the kitchen.

She was greeted with many hellos, including Jace. "Hey, Hanna. Good morning."

"Morning, Jace. How are you?"

"I'm good. Today's the day. The big fishing tournament starts. So glad to see you with fresh buns."

She chuckled. "Thanks, Jace. I hope you guys knock it out of the park with sales today."

"You and me both, lady. You and me both."

She set the buns on the stainless-steel table in the kitchen and went back for more. Her phone vibrated in her pocket and a sour taste filled her mouth. Not another one, or maybe the same one. She wasn't quite sure, but she didn't want to talk to any of them.

She carried a couple more racks of buns into the kitchen. Jace followed her out to help her. "So you've made my friend quite the happy man. Every time I see him now, he whistles."

Hanna chuckled. "Well, I'm glad to hear that. Better than the opposite, right?"

Jace laughed. "That's right. You have no idea what that poor man went through with that awful ex-wife of his. I'm so glad he's happy."

"Well, it appears we have a lot in common. We've both been through some unsavory things, we both own a business, and we're close to the same age, so I guess we understand each other."

"True that," Jace said.

She waved goodbye to Jace and got into her SUV to leave. Sucking in a deep breath, she decided to be brave and check her phone and see who it was that had called. Her tummy rolled when she saw the name on the readout, but this time it was actually more like butterflies. It was Quinn.

She tapped her text messages and read. "Hey, you won't believe what's going on here. We're already demoing the barracks and the architect thinks that we can easily make this into condos. Happy day."

She smiled as she read, sent him the little kiss emoji, and headed back toward the bakery. She had a weird feeling someone was watching her, but as she looked around, she didn't see anything, so she just chalked it up to being paranoid. All these women coming out of the woodwork seemed to just irritate her. It was making her feel weird, although she had no reason to feel weird. Just as she was walking into the bakery, her phone rang again. "My god, today is *call Hanna day* with my phone," she mumbled. She hung her purse on the hook near the kitchen and checked her phone.

Tisha. She answered quickly, "Hi, Tisha. How are you?"

"I'm doing well. Just calling to check and make sure

that you received the flooring that my son dropped off, and to see if it's going to work out in your house."

Hanna's cheeks burned. She had barely noticed the flooring this morning when she had gotten home. "I'll be honest with you. I didn't have much of a chance to look at it. I had a date last night and ended up coming back here to work and spent the night here, so when I went home this morning to shower, I really only stepped over the flooring that was stacked on the floor. I didn't get the chance to look at it, but I'll make sure to look at it tonight."

"Not a problem. I just wanted to make sure it had gotten there, and that you were happy with it. So, who was your date with?"

Hanna's cheeks burned again, only this time for a different reason. "Can I just say I'm not ready to say yet?"

Tisha chuckled. "Yes, you can say that. That's fine. I just thought I'd check, and please let me know if you have any problems with the table and the flooring."

"Will do, Tisha. Thank you for understanding."

"I do. I also just wanted to chat with you. I haven't seen you in a few days and..." She trailed off and Hanna leaned against the stainless-steel counter in her kitchen.

"Is everything alright, Tisha?"

"Yes. I'm sorry I shouldn't bother you. We don't really know each other that well."

Hanna felt bad. This woman didn't have any friends. "I'm not bothered by you calling and if you need to talk, I'm happy to talk to you."

"It's just that I feel like I'm being followed lately. Does that seem overly paranoid?"

Hanna's heart sped up. She'd been feeling the same way. That was an awfully weird coincidence. "No, that isn't paranoid at all. Have you noticed anyone following you?"

"No, that's what makes it seem foolish."

"Tisha. It isn't foolish. If you have that feeling, it's valid. Please be very aware of your surroundings and if you feel at all threatened, you need to get some security."

"I will. Thank you for not making me feel foolish."

Hanna shook her head. "You are not foolish. I'm glad you told me. Are you alright now?"

"Yes. I won't keep you. Please let me know when you see the table in your place and take a look at the flooring in your house. Sometimes things look different in other lighting."

"I promise you I will let you know as soon as I get home."

Quinn hopped out of his truck and sauntered into the flower shop. He looked around at the displays they had, and an older lady behind the counter asked him, "How can I help you today?"

He grinned. "I'd like to bring flowers to my girlfriend."

She smiled. "Okay, well we can certainly help you with that. So tell me, is it apology flowers or I love you flowers or something to celebrate a special occasion?"

His heart beat faster. They hadn't said the L word to each other, and until right now, he hadn't even let himself think along those lines. Taking it day by day is his motto.

He said, "Well, I didn't do anything wrong yet, so it's not for an apology. Mostly, I just want to let her know I'm thinking about her."

"Oh, well, that's a beautiful reason to give your girlfriend flowers. So let me show you some of the options that we have." She plodded over to a cooler with some floral bouquets inside. She slid the door open and pulled out a bouquet. "We have these beautiful sunflowers.

They're very bright and cheery. Sure, to make anybody happy."

"I like those. And you're right, they're bright and happy and cheery. That's just how she makes me feel. I'll take that bouquet right there."

The older lady smiled and put her hand to her heart. "Aren't you just the sweetest?" She wrapped them up with pretty tissue paper, tucked in some baby's breath, and made the bouquet look absolutely wonderful.

He grinned as he stared at it. "That's perfect. Thank you."

He paid for the flowers and exited the flower shop, feeling better than he'd felt in years. Literally years.

Quickly driving over to Hanna's bakery, he sauntered in with a huge smile on his face. His cheeks stretched, and he wasn't sorry.

Hanna was behind the counter, helping an older lady. The instant she looked up and saw him, her smile lit up the entire room. She was stunning.

The little lady she was helping, grabbed her bag and shuffled past him. She looked at the flowers and smiled. "Those are beautiful."

He nodded. "Thank you so much."

Stepping up to the counter, he handed the flowers to Hanna.

"This is just to let you know I've been thinking about you, and that you make me feel happy."

She giggled. "Oh my gosh, they're beautiful. Thank you. Thank you so much for making my day."

He grinned, "Well, actually, the thank you is mine. Thank you for making my day."

Hanna kept glancing out the window. And at one

point, she thought she heard the back door open and jumped.

"Is everything okay, Hanna?"

"Yeah. Yeah." Her shoulders dropped. "I'm sure everything is just fine."

"Well, now that doesn't sound convincing at all. Why don't you tell me what's got you spooked?"

"Uh, you're going to think it sounds stupid."

"I'm not going to think it sounds stupid. Let me be the judge of that. Now tell me what has you rattled."

She took a couple deep breaths and looked at the top of the counter rather than his eyes. His stomach began to twist a little. She was obviously worried about something.

Finally, he said, "Hanna, why don't you let me help you?"

She sighed, letting out her breath, and said, "Well, it's really silly, but I feel like someone's watching me. It feels so weird."

He said, "Did somebody make you feel like they were watching you?"

"No, that's not it. See, I told you it sounded weird, but it's just..." she shrugged. "I don't know. I've just had this weird feeling all morning that someone was watching me."

"Okay. Well, do you need me to stay here for a while until you're finished with your day to make sure you're okay?"

"No. I mean...nothing's happened where I should feel this way. I don't know. I guess all this stuff with Isaac has just made me a little uneasy, and I don't know, I'm just going to try not to let it get to me."

He stepped forward and took her hands in his. "Hey, if

you need me to stay, I can stay. If you need some assistance, I can find a cop to come and watch the place for you. And if you need to leave for the day, I'm sure your customers will understand. Tell me what you need and let me help you."

She squeezed his hands and looked into his eyes. "You know, you really are a nice man."

He said, "Well, I'm glad you feel that way. I think you're a nice woman."

She laughed, and he squeezed her fingers. "That's what I was looking for. So tell me what you need, and let me help you."

"I'm fine, really, I'm fine. And what I need right now is to put these beautiful flowers in water and let them grace my counter. They're stunning. Thank you so much."

He grinned. "That's what I was looking for. I was looking for that beautiful smile of yours."

"I'm sorry to be a downer. I didn't mean to do that. It's just, I don't know, you know, how some days are better than others."

"That I do." He grinned.

"All right. So today is just one of those days, I guess."

He said, "Well, let me help you with that, too. How about after work tonight, we have a nice, quiet dinner? I previously texted about a picnic on the beach, but I can try to cook at my place instead."

She laughed. "You want to cook dinner for me?"

"Well, I said I would try to cook dinner. I'm not the best cook. Actually, Jace is the cook of my friends' group, but I've learned a couple things over time. I think I can manage an easy dinner if you're open to something simple."

She chuckled, "Simple is fine with me, and quite frankly, I'm more than happy to cook for you."

"Well, you cook all day. Bake anyway, which is sort of the same thing, but not. Let me do something for you. How about I pick you up tonight around six o'clock and bring you back to my place, and we'll have dinner?"

"That sounds like you have to make dinner, then put everything on hold to come and pick me up, and then take me back. So how about if I just meet you at your place at six o'clock?"

He grinned. Then looked around. There was no one in the bakery at this moment, so he leaned forward and kissed her lips lightly.

"That sounds like a great date. I'll see you at six."

She smiled. "That sounds good. I'm looking forward to it."

He turned and walked toward the door, but not before turning and winking at her.

Hopping in his truck, he felt elated, and now he was going to go over and ask Jace what he could make because he didn't really cook all that much.

He wanted to try and impress Hanna, but he was also not opposed to cheating a little bit to impress her. He turned his truck toward the Sandbar.

Feeling light-hearted, he pulled in the Sandbar parking lot and strode inside the front door.

Jace was cleaning the bar. "Hey, bud."

"Hey, Quinn. How are you?"

"I'm good. So I have a date tonight, and I need something quick and simple to make that, you know, something that I can make."

Jace laughed. "How about this? How about if I make you a nice dinner and package it up, and then you just swing by and pick it up? All you'll have to do is warm it up, put it on nice dishes, and voilà."

"That's the best plan I've heard all day," Quinn laughed.

"All right. Glad to help. I'll have something prepared for you around, what, five-thirty? But I'm going to make it a surprise."

"That's okay. Just don't make it too complicated so Hanna can possibly think that I made it."

Jace shook his head. "Well, I'm not going to promise you that, but I'll promise you a great meal."

"Well, I guess I can live with a great meal."

He hopped back in his truck and headed toward the barracks. He felt so much promise for the future.

The back door opened and Hanna jumped. She popped her head out of the kitchen and looked down the hall to see her mom.

"Hi, honey, I thought I'd come and help out a little bit today. I understand you had an extra big bun order, and I thought maybe other things were set on the back burner."

Hanna's heartbeat raced, and she cleared her throat lightly, giving herself a moment to settle.

"Thanks, Mom, yeah a couple things got put on the back burner. I need to get some cookies in the oven. If you wouldn't mind rolling those out, I'd appreciate it. I have the dough all ready to go in the fridge. And then I can work on another batch of cinnamon rolls."

"Sounds good, sweetheart. Dad told me that he invited you to dinner the other night and you couldn't make it, but we would like you to come to dinner tonight."

Hanna froze. Now, what did she do? She was in a relationship, right? Small town, word was going to get out, eventually. She probably better tell her parents before they heard something through the grapevine. After all, they weren't exactly sneaking around.

She twisted her fingers together, "So Mom, I've been seeing someone. Just a few times. But well, I've been seeing someone, and I'm supposed to have dinner with him tonight."

Her mom stopped. Her smile spread across her entire face. Her dark hair was pulled back in a ponytail. Much like Hanna usually wore while she was at the bakery.

"Is that so? Well, we would of course like to meet him, and of course, he's invited tonight as well."

Hanna played with her fingers. "Well, I'd have to ask him if he wants to do that. We haven't talked about... you know, meeting the parents or anything... or the kids, or whatnot."

"So he has children."

"Yes, he has two children. They're both grown. I mean, at my age, you know, that's who I'm going to meet, somebody with children likely."

"Oh honey, thank God you didn't have children with that criminal that you were married to."

"I know Mom, I know, I know, I know. I've thought of it so many times myself I can't tell you. That doesn't mean I don't wish I did have them, though."

"Well, you know with modern medicine and everything it's still not too late. You're only forty-five."

"Well, I'm not talking about having children, Mom. My gosh that's...oh my gosh I can't even think of that right now. But if the good Lord wants it I guess it could happen. Anyway, I'm not anywhere near that time, talking about that or anything. We're not that serious. But let me call him and ask him if he's interested in having dinner with you and Dad."

"Well, tell him we're interested in meeting him. And who is this him, anyway? So I don't have to keep calling him, *him*."

Hanna chuckled. "His name is Quinn Kurtz. And he..."

"Oh, I know Quinn Kurtz. Oh my goodness he's such a handsome man. You're lucky. He's, ooh, what do the girls call him these days? Dreamy?"

"Mom!"

"Well, he is, right? Dreamy."

"Yes, he's dreamy, but you shouldn't think that way about him. I mean what would Dad think?"

"Oh, honey your father and I have been married so many years he knows when I think a man is dreamy. I'll even tell him tonight that we're having dinner with the dreamy Quinn Kurtz."

Hanna's cheeks heated. "Well, I don't know that yet. I have to call him."

"Then you call him while I'm rolling out these cookies and get that taken care of. We'll grill steaks. Your dad is really good at grilling steaks."

"Okay, well, don't get too far ahead of yourself. Let me give Quinn a call and see if he's even interested. He was planning on cooking for me tonight."

Her mom scoffed. "How could he not be interested? If he likes you at all, he's going to want to meet your family to see where you come from."

Hanna chuckled and walked out into the front of the bakery. It was quiet right now, so it was a good time to call him.

She pulled her phone out of her back pocket and tapped his number.

"Hey there, beautiful. Good to hear from you."

His voice was so happy and cheerful that it brought a smile to her face. "Well, you may not think so in a minute."

"Uh oh, what's going on?"

"Nothing's going on, but my mom is kind of insisting that you come over tonight and have dinner with them. I know we haven't talked about meeting my parents, but is that something that you might be interested in?"

Quinn laughed. "Well, first of all I know your parents, sort of. In passing mostly in and out of church, at weddings. Small town, you know."

"Right yeah, I know." She laughed.

"But I don't see why that wouldn't work. Yeah, let's do it. Why don't we have dinner with your parents tonight? I'd love to meet them. What are they having? I'll bring wine and some flowers for your mom. How about that?"

Hanna laughed. "You'll turn her head. She already thinks you're dreamy."

He laughed out loud, and the sound made butterflies take flight in her tummy. She smiled as she listened to the melodic sound.

"Dreamy huh?"

"Yes, those were her exact words. As a matter of fact, when I asked her what Dad would think, she said, 'Honey I will tell him I'm having dinner tonight with the dreamy Quinn Kurtz.'"

He laughed again and she closed her eyes to focus on the sound. And then it dawned on her that she'd had little laughter in her life with Isaac. This was so... well it was so darn nice.

"Yes, okay, well, I don't know that I want to play that up too much, but I'll pick up flowers and wine. I'll pick you up at your house at six o'clock to meet the parents."

"Thank you so much, Quinn. I do appreciate you being

willing to change your plans for them, and on the spur of the moment. Sort of, at least formally."

He laughed again. "It's fine, hon it's fine. It'll be fun. Talk to you later, sweetheart."

"Talk to you later." She tapped the end call on her phone and her heart beat so hard in her chest she wondered if anyone else could hear it. Butterflies rolled around in her stomach. He called her *hon* and *sweetheart.* Things were starting to get a little real. She turned around and jumped.

Her mom was standing right there, listening.

"So I suppose you heard."

"Well no. I just... Well, so he's coming, right?"

Hanna laughed. "Yes, he's coming. Oh my god, Mom, you act like I've never had a boyfriend over before."

Her mom sighed. "You've never had a quality boyfriend, sweetheart."

And then it dawned on her that her mom called her sweetheart, too. Two times in one day. A girl could get used to that.

She went back into the kitchen to roll out her cinnamon rolls and get them ready for baking when her phone rang again.

"My god it's like everybody wants to talk to me today."

Her mom tsked. "Of course they do. You're Hanna, cinnamon roll girl, Valentine. Why wouldn't they want to talk to you?"

Her mom giggled at her own joke, and Hanna shrugged her shoulders and looked at her phone. It was her friend Jalyn.

"Hey, Jay. Nice to hear from you."

"Well, I haven't heard from you in a couple of days. I've been wondering what's going on."

"Well, nothing's going on. I mean, what do you mean what's going on?'

"I mean I haven't heard from you in a couple of days. I normally hear from you at least once every other day."

Hanna stopped to lean on the table. "Well, you know you could have called me sooner if you wanted to. What's going on with you that you haven't called?"

Jalyn was silent for a moment. She finally responded, "All right ya got me. Nothing's really going on. I was just sulking because you weren't calling me."

Hanna chuckled. "Well, that's stupid. Just call me when you want to call me. I've been a little busy. That's all. There's a big fishing tournament in town, so the Sandbar ordered extra buns for sandwiches. I have a lot of cinnamon rolls rolling out the door. No pun intended. And I've had a few dates with Quinn. Well, I guess maybe three."

"Three dates? Oh my God. Have you guys...have you...?"

"Stop it. Don't ask. My mom's here, by the way."

"Oh no, she can't hear me can she?"

"No, not really. She's trying to though." Hanna glanced at her mom. "Aren't you, mom? Trying to listen to what Jalyn's saying."

"I'm not. I'm not. I'm just rolling out these cookies. I'm not trying to overhear or eavesdrop or anything. You're standing right next to me."

Hanna laughed. "Anyway Jalyn, Quinn's coming over to my mom and dad's house tonight to meet the parents. So that's what's been going on."

"Oh my God. I would love to be there and see that."

"Tell her she's welcome to come and join us."

"So you can hear?"

Jalyn said, "Oh my God she can hear me?"

Hanna shook her head. "I don't know. She's got selective hearing, but I think she heard everything."

"Oh my God. I'll have to remember that next time I call. I'll ask if you're alone first. Apparently, it's a good question to ask since you're also dating Quinn Kurtz now."

"Stop it. Oh my God." She took a deep breath. "Anyway, dinner at six. Dad's making steaks for all of us. Quinn's bringing wine. Why don't you bring a dessert?"

"You want me to bring a dessert? You're the baker."

"I bake desserts all day long. If you don't want to bring a dessert, how about you bring, I don't know, an hors d'oeuvre."

"That I can do. I'll bring the hors d'oeuvre. I'll see you around six o'clock tonight. And tell your mom I said hi."

Her mom grinned and yelled, "Hi, Jalyn, I'll see you later."

Hanna shook her head as Jalyn laughed, then ended the call.

24

Quinn knocked on Hanna's door. If he was being honest with himself, he was excited about formally meeting Hanna's parents. Though he knew of them or about them for years. He didn't know they had a beautiful daughter that he'd one day be totally smitten with. For some reason, that changed things.

She opened the door and the smile he was greeted with nearly took his breath away.

"Hi, I hope you're ready for this." She chuckled.

He grinned. "I don't know what you're so nervous about. I've met your parents, though it was brief, and apparently your mom thinks I'm dreamy, so there should be no problems tonight unless your dad is going to take offense to that."

Hanna laughed. He watched her face transform into one of happiness and enjoyment. He couldn't look away. "He's not going to take offense to that. You're funny."

"Well, you shouldn't be nervous. I can be a perfect gentleman. I won't embarrass you, I promise."

"Oh my gosh, Quinn. I am not worried about you embarrassing me. I'm worried about them embarrassing you. I don't know what to think about all of this. They're so excited that I'm no longer with Isaac, and I'm just not sure how hard they're going to push it." She stepped back to let him inside. "Oh, and also, since we've spoken, my best friend, Jalyn, is going to be joining us, too. So, I'm sorry you're going to be grilled tonight. Hopefully, not as much as the steaks."

He laughed. Then he examined her living room and the piles of tools, paint cans, flooring, drywall, and other things she had lying around. "You really haven't had much time to get anything done here. Why don't you let me send a couple guys over? I won't charge you anything. They can get this floor banged out in a couple of days, get your trim work back up, and even help you paint. Then you don't have to live in a construction zone."

"I don't want to do that. You're busy with the barracks right now. Don't you have that to get done? And I don't want you to hold your schedule up in getting those rented to help me out."

"Well, I do have extra guys. And some of them don't always have a lot of work. I've got a couple guys I can put on this job. It'll keep them busy, and I don't have to worry about them going out and looking for other jobs because they're not working."

She looked around the room at all the stuff and quietly responded. "Quinn, I don't know. It seems like it's an awful lot to ask of you."

"As I recall, you didn't ask. I offered, and just so you know, when Sid and Grace got together, I sent Jared and another fellow over to help Grace put her flooring in and to put some new windows in. I did it all pro bono. And she was able to get her place up and running in no time. She rents it out now, that one and another over by the water. I'll show you the next time we go over to the Sandbar."

"Um, okay." He saw her cheeks tint a pretty pink and felt bad that she seemed embarrassed, but he really did want to help her. "Well, it's not that I don't trust your work because I certainly do. But let me think about it. I just don't want to feel like I'm taking advantage of you."

"Oh," he leaned in, and kissed her lips softly, a few times. Then he whispered, "Take advantage of me all you want, sweetheart." He wanted her to take advantage of him. He looked forward to it, actually.

They got into his truck and headed toward her parents' house.

Hanna glanced out the side window and a couple of times she turned to look behind them.

"Honey, are you still feeling like someone's following you?"

"I'm sorry. I know it seems like I'm being overly paranoid, but it's the weirdest thing. I do feel like someone's just kind of watching. But I never see anybody when I look around."

He was quiet for a moment, worried that maybe all the stress from Isaac was finally getting to her. He didn't want to say that out loud because that sounded quite bold and insensitive. And yet she was genuinely worried.

"Well, my offer still stands. If you need me to stay close, I'm happy to do that. I mean, really happy to do that, if you know what I mean."

She laughed, and he enjoyed the sound. It felt good to make her laugh. He felt powerful in the sense that he could alter her mood in a positive way.

"So tell me what I'm going to need to know about your

best friend or your parents so that I don't put my foot in my mouth tonight."

She grinned. "You won't put your foot in your mouth. Really, there's nothing to know. My dad was an accountant in his pre-retirement life, and he did the books for the bakery for my grandmother, my mother, and now me. He's happily retired. He's a golfer, and he likes to be out on their pontoon boat. Mom doesn't mind being on the pontoon boat, but she likes it less than Dad. Mom ran the bakery for many, many years. She inherited it from her mother, and that's kind of my parents."

"My best friend, Jalyn, she's another story. She's been my best friend all through school, and when we both went off to college, we went together. She was married and divorced, and she is the first female firefighter in Blossom Springs. Her father was a firefighter as well. She's quite impressive. Tall. Thin. She has green eyes and long dark hair, and she really -- if it's on her mind, she says it, so don't be shocked."

He laughed. "Well, that is impressive." His brows furrowed, "The first female firefighter, wow. Is that what she always wanted to do?"

"No, but I'll let her tell you the story. And hopefully she won't get a fire call tonight because it seems like she's always on call. You know, there aren't a lot of firefighters in Blossom Springs, being a small town and all. So anyway, I'll let you be the judge."

He chuckled. "Okay, it's funny. I haven't heard of that first female firefighter in Blossom Springs, and I guess I should be grateful that I don't have to know that. I haven't needed to call the fire department, so that's good."

"That's real good." She added.

They pulled up to her parents' house. He ran around,

opened the door for her, then reached into the backseat and pulled out a bottle of wine in a gift bag, and a bouquet of red, white, and blue carnations.

Hanna smiled brightly. "She's going to love those."

"That's good. And I think I'm the new favorite at the flower shop today."

Hanna laughed. "Well, I do want to say thank you again. They sure did brighten my day."

"That was the point," he said.

As they reached the front door, Hanna opened it and stepped inside, grabbing his hand and pulling him with her.

"Mom, Dad, we're here."

25

anna introduced Quinn to her parents. "Quinn, this is my mother, Allison. Mom, this is Quinn Kurtz. This is my father, Lance." They shook hands. "Quinn says he's met you in passing, but never formally, so consider yourselves introduced.

Quinn handed her mom the bottle of wine and the flowers. "It's very nice to meet both of you. You have an incredible daughter."

Hanna's cheeks warmed slightly. She wasn't used to being complimented in front of her parents by a man. It was certainly a new experience, and one she rather liked.

Her father chuckled. "Well, come on in. Let's get us some drinks. What are you drinking, Quinn?"

Quinn laughed. "Beer is just fine with me, sir."

"I haven't been *sir* for a long time. How about Lance?"

Quinn nodded and smiled. "Lance it is."

Hanna looked over at her mother who stood staring. Was her mouth open? Oh my god, she was gaping at him like she'd never seen a handsome man before. Hanna nudged her mom. "Should we go put these flowers in some water, Mom?"

Her mom tittered a little. "Oh yes. Oh, gosh, yes of course. Yes, thank you, Quinn. Oh, they're so beautiful. I just can't believe how sweet you are."

Hanna looked at Quinn and grinned, then she slipped her arm under her mom's arm and led her to the kitchen. "Oh my god, Mom. Seriously, get yourself together."

"Oh, but he's even dreamier up close. I had no idea, honey."

Hanna groaned. Well, her mom wasn't wrong, but oh my god, she wasn't expecting this reaction and it was a little embarrassing. She pulled the vase out of the cupboard and began cutting the stems of the flowers, while her mom set the bottle of wine on the counter.

"Oh, so thoughtful that he bought the red, white, and blue carnations. I mean with summer here and everything that is really just so patriotic and nice."

Hanna chuckled. "Well, he's a veteran, so of course he'd be patriotic, and he just thought they were bright and colorful. I guess the ladies at the flower shop are very enamored with him today for buying two bouquets."

"Two? He bought two bouquets?"

"Yes, he brought one to me earlier today at the bakery. Sunflowers. They're beautiful. Stop in and see them tomorrow if you like."

"Oh, oh maybe I'll do that. Oh, he's so nice, he's just so sweet.

Hanna chuckled. "Oh my gosh, Mom, get yourself together."

They arranged the flowers and her mom happily put them in the center of the dining room table when Jalyn walked in. "Hey, everybody I'm here."

Hanna rushed out to the living room and hugged her friend then turned around and introduced her to Quinn. "Quinn this is my best friend Jalyn. Jalyn meet Quinn."

She leaned in closer and whispered, "And don't make a fool of yourself. My mom has been tittering and tottering.

Jalyn chuckled. "Of course, she is."

"Hi, Quinn, nice to meet you." She held out her hand and shook his vigorously, then she looked at Hanna. "Are we drinking beer tonight?"

"Aren't you on call?"

"Not tonight. I asked for the night off so I'm primed and ready to have a couple beers, a good dinner, and meet this man that you've been spending so much time with that you don't even have time to call me."

"Jalyn, we've talked about this already."

"I know, I know, I know. I could call you, too, but well...."

"Good Lord." Hanna sighed quietly, so she didn't offend anyone, but she was a little perplexed at how this evening had already started.

Quinn chuckled, then had a conversation with her dad about business, which she thought was kind of cute, and then he told her parents and Jalyn about the barracks project and what they were doing there. They were all excited about what he was planning to do, and all agreed that the property needed some sprucing up, so this was going to be a good thing for the town.

Her dad said, "All right I'm going to get the steaks on the grill.

Quinn stood up with him, "I'll help you."

The two men in her life walked out of the room together, and she thought it was rather sweet.

Her phone rang, and she pulled it from her pocket and saw Isaac's number. She closed her eyes as Jalyn looked over and saw who was on the phone. "Don't answer that."

Not wanting to speak to Isaac anyway, she tapped the phone and hung up the call. It wasn't even a minute later, and the phone rang again. Isaac again. She stood and walked out of the room. "I might as well answer it, or he'll just keep calling." She answered her phone, "Yes, Isaac, how can I help you today?"

She shouldn't have offered to help him at all. He'd take advantage of that if he could.

"Can we... can we talk? Can I, can I, can we meet together and talk?"

"No."

"No? You won't talk to me?"

"I don't want to talk to you, Isaac. I would think the divorce would have been a pretty good sign of that."

"But I'm in town now, and I just want to meet you for a little while. I just want to apologize."

"You can apologize on the phone and then that's it. I'm at Mom and Dad's tonight and I don't want to have this conversation with you, like ever."

"Hanna, please just let me meet you in person and talk to you. I just want to say I'm sorry and I just want to see your face so that you believe me."

"Isaac, I don't believe I will ever believe you again. I don't want to have this conversation with you now, or ever, and I don't need your apology. I'm over it. I'm over it all. Please don't call again."

"But,Hanna, please."

She hung up the phone, took in a deep breath, and let it out slowly. After a moment, she sauntered back into the living room where Jalyn and her mom sat waiting for her.

"He's in town apparently and wanted to talk to me. He wanted to apologize. I told him he could apologize on the phone. He didn't want to do that. He begged. I said no that's the end of it. I'm not meeting with him. I'm not talking to him. I don't want to have anything to do with him, to be honest with you. So, hopefully, that's the last I will hear from him tonight."

"Well, let's hope so," her mom said. "Besides, it doesn't look good when you're taking calls from your ex-husband when you're here with your new boyfriend."

"I've already told Quinn all about Isaac, and all the crap he's pulled, and his recent shenanigans. He's aware of what kind of person Isaac is. But I tend to agree with you. I don't want Isaac intruding on any of my time with Quinn. Actually, I don't want Isaac intruding on any of my time, period, so I won't be taking any more of his calls."

Her father and Quinn walked back into the house with a plate of delicious-smelling steaks.

"Steaks are ready."

Her mom jumped up. "Okay, let's go. It's time to eat."

Her mom hustled about, refreshing everyone's drinks. Then, they sat down and had a nice meal.

Dinner conversation centered around the new stage the Sandbar was building. The new flower pots the business league purchased for each Main Street business so there was a cohesive look to the street. And the upcoming election and the two mayoral candidates.

Quinn made it very easy for her parents to talk to him about anything. He was engaging, open, and honest.

And happily, they were all on the same page politically, so she could breathe a sigh of relief. Quinn asked Jalyn about being the first female firefighter. And he asked her questions about Hanna, which she was a bit uncomfortable with, but they laughed. Jalyn had a couple cute stories which Quinn seemed to enjoy. Then her phone rang.

Her mother sat up straight. Hanna looked over at her phone to see who it was, but it wasn't a number she recognized.

She moved away from the table. Her mom had a strict 'no phones at the table' policy. As she moved into the living room, she tapped the green icon on her phone. "Hello."

No one was there. "Hello?" A few seconds more and she said, "Hello?" Shrugging her shoulders she ended the call and thought that was the end of it, but it rang again. This time, it was a different number. "Hello? Hello? Hello?"

She ended the call and sat at the table once more. She was seated at a right angle to Quinn and next to Jalyn. "I don't know why someone's calling and not talking to me. It was a different number both times."

Her mom leaned forward. "Honey, are you sure it's not Isaac trying to call again?"

Quinn turned his head to her. "Isaac called?"

"Yes, while you and Dad were grilling. He wanted to talk. I told him no, and not to call me anymore. Apparently, he's in town."

"Okay, and you're sure those calls aren't from him?"

"They're not his number."

"Okay, well we'll see what happens with it." He reached across the corner of the table and placed his hand over hers.

Her phone rang again, and she jumped.

This time, Quinn leaned over. "May I?"

She handed him the phone. "Have at it."

He answered the phone. "Hello, this is Quinn." He listened. He didn't say anything further. He finally said, "Rather than this cowardly act why don't you act like a man? If you have something to say, say it. If not, this harassment is illegal as hell on a phone according to the FCC. Keep it up; you'll find out." The call ended. He turned off her phone and handed it back to her. "How do you feel about just keeping it off for the rest of the night so we can enjoy ourselves?"

"I'm fine with that." She put it in her back pocket and tried to relax. Her shoulders had stiffened up through all this nonsense, but maybe she and Quinn would have a way of working those out later. Her cheeks heated when she thought of that, and Jalyn leaned over and asked why she was blushing.

"It's nothing."

"I'll bet it's nothing," Jalyn teased.

"Stop it."

"Oh, I can't wait to hear why just sitting here next to Quinn makes you blush."

"Stop it."

Quinn chuckled. He nudged her foot under the table and she looked up at him. The grin on his face made her cheeks heat up even further. Her mom tittered across the table and she couldn't wait for this night to be over. My god it was as if her mom was possessed by another creature.

Her mom stood. "How about if we have dessert in the living room? I made a blueberry pie."

"That sounds great, Mom."

She and Jalyn got up and began clearing the dishes. Quinn carried his plate and some extra dishes into the kitchen and her mom looked at him, batted her eyelashes, and said, "Oh, that is so nice."

Hanna scoffed, "Oh my god, Mom. Quinn, go into the other room so she can't see you. Good lord."

He chuckled. Then he surprised the hell out of her by leaning down and kissing her lips. If her cheeks hadn't been red from before they sure were red now. Not only her cheeks, but the tips of her ears burned, and her chest was hot.

Jalyn had a Cheshire cat grin on her face.

Hanna wanted this part of the evening to be over. She was too tense from all this teasing, and the nonsense from her mom acting like a teenager. And why wasn't her father a bit irritated at that? It was like she didn't know any of these people anymore.

After dessert, they sat outside in the Florida room for an after-dinner drink. Lance made the best homemade Irish Cream. Maybe one day he'll try to make that. He'd never felt all that domestic, always looking for a reason to be away from home. But now he found himself thinking about making homemade Irish Cream, and perhaps he'd actually learn to cook a few dishes to help out. He grinned as they drove toward Hanna's place.

"What are you grinning about?" Hanna asked.

He chuckled. "I'd like to learn how to make Irish Cream."

"Dad does do a good job with that, doesn't he?"

"He certainly does."

Looking into the rearview mirror, he noticed a car coming up quickly behind him. He began watching in his rearview mirror regularly.

Turning right and taking an alternate route home, he watched as the vehicle continued to follow them.

Driving down First Street, he went past the Canning Ranch and pointed to it. "Does that look familiar to you?"

Hanna grinned. "It does. It actually looks the same."

He chuckled. "It does. They've done a lot of building further into the ranch, but from here it does look largely the same."

Finally getting a good view of the driver behind them, he recognized his ex. His jaw clenched when she turned to follow behind them. He sped up just a little bit and so did she. He'd deal with her later.

Hanna turned to look out the windows, then behind them to see the black Lexis. "Are they following us?"

"It sure feels like it."

He turned into Hanna's driveway, but before they got out, his ex slowed down and then sped up and took off.

Hanna said, "Who was that?"

He let out a deep sigh. "That was my ex. She followed us from your parents' place."

Hanna swallowed and her brows furrowed slightly. He hated seeing the worry on her face.

"Do you think it would have been her that called?"

"I don't know. Those numbers didn't seem like anything that I'd ever seen before. And, when I answered your phone, that should have jolted her to say something. Whoever was on the phone just breathed heavily and didn't say anything."

"Okay." Hanna turned to look out the back window. "Is she dangerous?"

"My ex? No, she's devious. She's manipulative, but I don't think she's dangerous."

"You don't think? I mean, could it bother her that she knows that we're dating? I mean, clearly, she knows now that we're dating. I mean, Jared probably said something, not to be mean, but he knows."

"Right. Well, I don't think she's dangerous and I will have a chat with her about following me, and to see if she's actually the person who was on the phone."

"Okay, but..." Hanna took a deep breath. Her fingers twisted together in her lap. Her voice was soft when she asked, "Will you stay with me tonight? I mean, I'm nervous. I'm a little creeped out here. Between Isaac and your ex and people calling and not saying anything and hanging up, I guess I'm a little rattled."

He twisted slightly in his seat and took her hand in his.

"Hanna, I'm sorry this is all happening right now. And if it's Tisha that's been calling you, and just trying to be generally a pain, I'll make that stop."

Hanna's eyes shot to his and held. Her mouth opened. Her brows shot up into her hairline. "Tisha? Tisha Barkley? Tisha is your ex-wife?"

"Tisha, yes. Tisha Barkley is my ex-wife. Do you know her?"

"I met her at the thrift store when I was looking to buy my bathroom vanity. And she was there to drop one off. And she gave it to me. She gave me her bathroom vanity."

"No kidding. I had no idea. And for the record, that's normally not like her. The giving spirit doesn't reside in her body."

"Well, I can't..." She swallowed again. "I can't say anything about that because she's been nice to me. She gave me some flooring. She gave me a table. I don't know if she thinks I'm a charity case or what. I suppose I looked pretty pathetic when I was trying to buy a thirty-five-dollar bathroom vanity and I couldn't. I didn't have enough money in my bank account because Isaac had drained my account. So she probably thinks I'm pitiful.

"And then she called and wanted to have lunch and that's when she gave me the table and the flooring, and... oh my god." She stopped and stared deeply into his eyes. "Oh, Quinn, I'm so sorry."

"What are you sorry for?"

"It was me. I'm the one who told her...oh no." She ran her hands down her cheeks. "I'm the one who told her I had a friend who got divorced, and her husband owned a business, and she took him back to court and got a percentage of his business in perpetuity. I'm so sorry. It's my fault. It's my fault she's taking you back to court."

Quinn swallowed as his heart hammered in his chest. He wasn't sure if Tisha was using Hanna or if it had been a happenstance thing. But something was definitely weird about this whole situation.

He reached his right hand up and cupped the side of her face. He smoothed his thumb over her cheekbone softly.

"Hanna, don't worry about it. It's not like you were trying to harm me in any way. You were just trying to help someone you thought was your friend. It's okay. It's all going to be just fine. However, it works out is how it works out. I'll deal with that, and you don't need to worry about it."

He took a deep breath and huffed it out. "In the meantime, how about this? How about if we go to my house for the night and stay there? I have security. No one can get onto the premises. Hopefully, you'll be able to sleep a little bit better knowing that you're safe there. Would that be alright with you?"

"Her eyes welled with tears and she sniffed daintily. "Are you sure? I wouldn't blame you if you were upset."

He shook his head. "I'm not upset."

"I would feel more comfortable at your place if you're sure."

"Honey, that's it. No more sorrys. It's okay. I know you weren't trying to harm me. You were just trying to help somebody. And that's fine. The bottom line is this. If I owe her money, I owe her money, and I'll pay it. But I don't want you worrying about it anymore. But know this. If you want to remain friends with Tisha, feel free to do that. But know that she's very manipulative. She's very conniving."

"Do you think she knew when she invited me over for lunch a few days ago that you and I were seeing each other? I mean, we had already had a date. She could have found out."

"I'm not sure about that. But don't worry about it. We'll find all that out in due time. For right now, do you need to go in and pack a bag?"

"Um, yeah." She let out a breath. "Yeah. If you don't mind, come in with me, please."

"I will, honey."

They entered the house and he could tell she was a little freaked out. He said, "Just stay right here. Let me check the house out."

He walked through the house to make sure there was no one in it. It was a small little bungalow so didn't take long. As he checked the bathroom, he noticed his former bathroom vanity was put in place. He just shook his head. What a weird set of situations this was.

He moved back to the living room. "All is fine, hon. Why don't you go ahead and pack your bag? I'll just wait out here for you."

Hanna moved down the hall. He watched her until she disappeared into the bedroom. Then he looked around at the items lying on the floor. He recognized the flooring, which he had ordered for Tisha's house. It wasn't much and would likely be enough to finish Hanna's living room and hallway.

He checked out the windows in the living room and didn't notice anyone driving by or sitting outside. That was a good thing. And, not for one minute did he think Tisha would make those calls. He wasn't sure why she followed them tonight or how she knew where he was. But he would find out.

27

Quinn opened the door for Hanna, and she stepped into his home. It was beautiful and had a masculine feel to it. Lots of brick and dark wood and leather. He closed and locked the door behind them, then set her bag on the floor near the door. He took her hand in his and led her to the first room past the kitchen.

"This is my office. I want to show you this."

He sat in the large leather chair behind the desk and shook his computer mouse. The monitor came to life. He entered his password, then clicked on a little blue icon.

"This is my security system."

A bunch of little squares populated the screen, each with a scene around the outside of his house.

"If someone breaks the plane of the cameras at the end of the driveway," he pointed to the square that showed the driveway, "I get a message on my phone, and the computer in here chimes, and the camera begins recording."

He pointed to the front door camera, the back door camera, and the Florida room camera. "All exits and entrances are covered. Plus, these additional cameras are monitoring the yard in the back and the fields."

She swallowed the lump in her throat as she looked at the cameras. It sure seemed secure.

"Are you paranoid?"

He laughed from deep in his belly. "I suppose it looks like it. But no. It's just that we had some trouble in town last year when an outlaw biker gang rolled in. So I installed these cameras for Sid and Grace, Jace, and myself. That gang was raising all kinds of hell and were especially targeting Sid and Grace because Sid refused to work on their bikes."

"Oh, wow. I hadn't heard about that."

"I'm surprised your parents didn't mention it. They targeted several businesses in town. Everyone was on high alert."

"How did you get rid of them?"

He turned his chair toward her and pulled her down on his lap. She wrapped her right arm around his shoulders and settled in. She liked sitting on his lap. The aroma of his aftershave surrounded her and the warmth of being pressed to him was comforting. She felt secure.

"Grace read up on the municipal code of conduct. She then wrote an amendment to the code of conduct to allow police to restrict troublemakers from creating havoc. Before that, until they actually broke a law, and the police had evidence, not much could be done. To get the emergency meeting, she needed enough signatures on a petition to ask for the meeting. Jace held a concert at the Sandbar, Hart & the Hurricanes played, and we asked everyone present to sign the petition for the emergency meeting. It was beautiful."

"Wow. That's fantastic. I can't wait to meet Grace."

He nodded and wrapped his arms around her, pulling her close. "I think we should call them and ask them to join us for dinner tomorrow. They're planning their wedding, so perhaps a break will be nice. Wanna be my date?"

She chuckled. "Sure. That will be our first big coming-out date. Jaws will be wagging."

He laughed and pulled her closer. "I can't wait."

She leaned in and kissed his lips. Softly. His were instantly eager for more and their kiss deepened quickly. His arms tightened around her and she enjoyed the feeling.

She pulled back. "Can I ask you a personal question?"

"Of course."

She took a deep breath. "Tisha said she stayed home and raised the kids, and then her ex-husband, who I now know is you, threw her out like garbage. Would you tell me why you two divorced?"

He sat back and stared into her eyes. His smile came easily, and he seemed rather happy to share his side of the story.

"Tisha and I divorced because she is never happy. Every time the house is remodeled, she wants it done again. Every time one of her friends adds a new piece of furniture, Tisha has to have better. It has been going on for years. The last ten years of our marriage were not a happy time. We argued. We fought. She threatened divorce or public disgrace or you-name-it. She was going to do it unless she got her way. I finally got to the point that I couldn't take it anymore. So, I packed up, moved out, and filed for divorce. And as per her usual, she didn't make that easy either."

Hanna nodded. "Thank you for sharing that with me. It isn't how she made it sound."

"I don't doubt it at all. And for the record, her father is a businessman and she could easily work for him. She doesn't want to work because it won't look good to her friends, who do not work."

Hanna looked into his eyes. She smiled softly, then lay her hand against his cheek. "I'm sorry for bringing it up. I just wanted to make sure. You know, after my experience..."

He turned his head and kissed her hand then faced her. "I understand."

His hand slid under her blouse and found her breasts. He enjoyed squeezing and massaging first one, then the other. He lifted her bra and the feel of his work-roughened hand on her tender breasts was exciting. He played with her breasts, squeezing and fondling her until she wanted to rip off his clothes and feel all of his skin. She was so turned on just by his touch. His kisses were magnificent. His lips felt incredible against hers.

His hand left her breasts and slid under her knees. He quickly stood, cradling her in his arms, and without a word he carried her to the living room, through the kitchen, and out a back door.

In the Florida room, there were windows looking out over his property, a comfortable sectional sofa, and a fireplace, which honestly was not needed tonight. He set her on her feet, flipped a switch to turn on the ceiling fan then came back to her.

His fingers slowly began to unbutton her blouse, but she covered her hands with his. "Won't someone see us?"

He grinned, then spun her around and stood closely

behind her. So close, in fact, she could feel the rigidness of his cock pressed into her butt.

He dipped his head down so his lips were close to her ear. He licked the shell of her ear first, then softly said, "What do you see out there?"

Her eyes focused out the windows at a field. "I see a wooden fence painted black, and a small garden with tomato plants and squash. Beyond the fence, I see a couple of horses grazing in another field."

"Do you think the horses are going to watch us make love?"

She chuckled. "No."

His lips kissed down her jaw and along her neck to her shoulder. He repeated his soft kisses, and she closed her eyes to absorb the sensual feel of him.

Thunder rolled across the sky, a bolt of lightning lit the room briefly, and rain began to fall outside. It added something to the moment. The thickening air created a sultry ambiance in the room.

Once his lips met her ear, he whispered softly, "I want you so bad, Hanna. I crave you."

Those words did things to her body that nothing in the world had ever done. It was as if an electric current sizzled around her body, touching every nerve ending. Wetness pooled between her legs and her knees shook slightly.

"I want you too, Quinn."

His fingers reached around her body and continued to unbutton her blouse. He slowly pulled her blouse over her shoulders and tossed it onto the small table in front of the sectional. She felt his fingers brush up her bare back and within a second, her bra strap snapped open and his hands eagerly divested her of her bra.

The warm sultry air in this room and the ceiling fan blowing softly on her body made her nipples pebble tightly and Quinn's strong sure fingers unbuttoned and unzipped her slacks. As soon as her slacks were opened, his fingers slid inside her pants, under her panties, and found the most perfect spot to touch her.

Her hips pushed forward into his fingers, and she wanted more. Now.

"Quinn."

He kissed her ear again, slid his hand from her pants, and spun her around once more so she was now facing him. He quickly pulled his shirt over his head, undid his pants, and slid them off while she watched him.

He was magnificent. His rigid cock strained toward her. His tanned body was toned, and his chest was peppered with just the perfect amount of dark and silver hair, which she found incredibly sexy. Her fingers dove into his chest hair, enjoying the feel of the curls against her skin. While she explored his body, he pushed her slacks and panties over her hips and let them fall.

Her fingers slid down his chest and her hand wrapped around his hardened cock, which made his breathing come in spurts.

He pushed into her hand back and forth a few times until the pre-cum glistened on top. She swiped her thumb over the pre-cum and smeared it over his cock, and she heard his breath hitch.

She stepped out of her slacks, pooled at her feet, and he swiftly picked her up and carried her to the sectional. He sat with her on his lap, then twisted and lay on his back.

"Ride me."

Her breath hitched, and the rawness of this moment

would always be carved into her brain because it was, without a doubt, the sexiest moment in her entire life.

She lifted herself over him, her knees on either side of his hips. She reached down and slid her hand up and down his cock a few times, then positioned the head of it at her entrance. She pushed down slightly, enough to insert the head of his cock into her, then she lay both of her hands on his chest and stared into his eyes.

His were dark and so intensely focused on her that she paused a moment. As they stared at each other, she slowly lowered herself onto him. A feeling she'd never, ever forget. She couldn't look away from his eyes as they bore into hers, and once she was seated fully, she wiggled herself around on him, then slowly lifted. She continued slowly until her own body betrayed her and demanded more.

Quinn's hands alternated between her breasts and her hips, sometimes holding her hips tightly to his body as she sat on him, to her bouncing breasts as her pace increased.

Their skin glistened with sweat as their exertion increased. Her hair stuck to the sides of her face as she rode him. She rode him hard.

She felt that first wave of need slide up her body, and she knew her climax was roaring to the end. Every nerve seemed to be on fire. Every hair seemed to stand on end. Her hearing dulled and her vision dimmed until all she could see was a pair of sexy dark brown eyes staring into hers as that white-hot pain turned to pleasure and she gasped her release as she said his name, "Quinn."

His hands gripped her hips and held her in place as he pushed tightly into her two more times and growled out her name. "Hanna."

Quinn woke more sated than he'd been...well, in his entire life.

Hanna lay curled up next to him, his arm around her body, and he liked the way he felt right now, this moment, and always with her. He liked having her near him. He liked having her sleep with him.

And he really liked making love to her. She rolled over and smiled. Her hair was tousled, her sleepy eyes stared into his. His heart thumped so loud he thought maybe she could hear it.

She leaned up and kissed his lips. "Do you want me to make you some breakfast?"

He stretched. "Well, it doesn't seem very nice of me to bring you over here and then make you cook."

"Well, you're not making me. I'm happy to do it. And besides, your kitchen is lovely. I'd love nothing more than to putter around in it for a while."

He chuckled. "All right, well, you go ahead and putter away. I'm gonna jump in the shower."

He kissed her lips again and then slid out of bed and walked toward the bathroom. Just before he stepped into the bathroom, he saw her scoot off the bed and stretch. Now that was a lovely sight. She was cute in the morning. She was cute all the time, but she was really cute in the morning. He jumped in the shower before his cock had other ideas, and tried to get his thoughts on today. He was going to find out what the hell Tisha was up to. Then he'd call Sid, to see if they'd want to have dinner with them tonight. And then he'd head off to the barracks to see how they were doing with the demolition.

After his shower, he dressed and headed out to the kitchen. The delicious aroma of eggs and bacon cooking called to him.

His stomach growled. "That smells delicious."

Hanna turned and smiled. She was wearing one of his t-shirts and damned it didn't look adorable on her. It hung down to her knees, but she didn't have a bra on, and her nipples pushed out the fabric in just the right way. He'd never look at that t-shirt the same again.

"Thank you. Do you like coffee in the morning?"

"I do."

"Good." She poured him a cup. "Cream, sugar, both, none?"

He chuckled. "Cream only. Thank you."

She set the creamer in front of him and then turned to the stove to turn the bacon in the pan.

They ate breakfast. Hanna took a shower, put on clean clothes, and then they took off in his vehicle.

They drove to her place. "So you're sure you want to meet Sid and Grace tonight? I'll call Sid and see if they're available."

"Yes, of course. I'd love to meet them."

"Sounds good. Also, just so you know, I'm going to have a discussion with Tisha today to find out what the hell she was doing."

Hanna's shoulders dropped a little bit. "Okay, well, I'm nervous about that, but..."

"What are you nervous about?"

"I just hope she wasn't playing me. I'm going to feel like such a fool."

"Well, we'll see what she's got to say. Don't worry about anything until I speak with her."

He pulled into her driveway and carried her bag inside. She could have done it herself, but he wanted to check her place, make sure it was okay, and at least give her the feeling that she was secure. And he liked doing things for her.

"Are you sure you don't want me to stay and follow you to the bakery?"

She chuckled. "No, I'm fine. You go ahead. You've done so much already."

He checked each room in her house. "All clear, sweetheart." He kissed her lips quickly, wrapped his arms around her, and held her close. Stepping back, he kissed her once more and strode out the door.

His thoughts now turned dark as he thought about talking to Tisha. On the ride up to her place, he tried keeping his anger in check. His thoughts were stormy. He assumed she was probably waiting for him to show up, anyway. He pulled into the driveway, marched up to the front door, and knocked firmly three times.

She opened the door and stared at him. She crossed her arms over her chest, and cocked a hip to the side. "What do you want?"

"Well, Tisha, I want to know why you were following

me last night, and how in the hell you knew that I was at Hanna's parents' place?"

He pushed past her to go inside, which was so not like him, but he was irritated as hell, and he wasn't going to give her the opportunity to slam the door in his face.

He stood in the foyer, hands in his pockets, trying to look casual, but his eyes bore into hers. "Well?"

She huffed out a deep breath. "For Christ's sake, Jared told me that you were seeing her, and I happened to see you driving with her in your truck last night, so I followed you. And when I saw where you were going, I decided to hang out and see how long you were there. So I parked at the end of the road."

"So you sat down at the end of the road for nearly three hours watching the Valentine's house just to see how long I was going to be there? You didn't have anything else to do but sit and wait."

She sucked in an irritated breath. "I didn't have anything else to do, no. And yes, I sat there, and I watched."

"Have you been following Hanna?"

"No."

She said she feels like someone's been following her. "Well, I haven't. I mean, well once I did."

"So you were following her?"

"I said once. Once I did."

"Tisha, for crying out loud..."

"Look, this is new. We've been divorced for five years. You haven't dated anyone significantly in all that time. A couple dates here and there, but that was it. And this is different, and I don't know. I just, I don't know, I guess I, it's different."

A light wind would have blown him over right now.

"How in the ever-loving fuck do you know I've had any dates? Are you following me?"

Tisha shrugged, which made him want to chew glass.

"All right, so it's different. But five years, Tisha, five years we've been divorced."

"I know, I know, I know it."

He sucked in a deep breath. "So tell me this. Did you know that Hanna and I had been dating when you invited her over for lunch last week?"

He watched her suck her lips into her mouth. Her eyes darted around the room, but not at him. And he knew the answer before she finally said it. But he stood there and waited. She needed to say it.

"Yes, I did. Jared told me that he thought you were dating, and so I called her to see if she wanted to have lunch. As a matter of fact, she told me she had had a date, but she wouldn't tell me with who. And so I felt like she was hiding something from me or being dishonest because, after all, she was dating my ex-husband."

"Well, Tisha, she didn't know until last night I was your ex-husband. How about that? She wasn't hiding anything from you."

"That's ridiculous. This is a small town. Everybody knows everybody."

"Well, she hasn't been in town for a while. You changed back to your maiden name, Barkley. She had no way of knowing. And for the record, she's not nosy enough to check around and see who was married to who, when, and for how long while she was gone. Unlike you, she has a lot to do. She's running a business. She doesn't have time to sit on somebody's street for three fucking hours and watch what they're doing."

"Oh, knock it off. It was one time. Big deal, so what?"

"Yeah, big deal, so what? Stop following me, and for fuck's sake, you better not follow her. And also, no more house renovation projects. Not from my pocketbook, anyway. You want to do it? Do it on your own. If you're gonna take me back to court to get some money from me, it's all on your own dime now. Got that?"

"Yes, I've got it. Fine."

"And I told Hanna, I don't have a problem if you two want to be friends. It makes it easier on the kids if you are, but I've told her that you are manipulative and deceitful. So if you're expecting to get any information from her about our relationship, know this. It won't happen. If you want to know something about my relationship, you ask me and me only. And if I think it's something that you need to know, I will tell you. If not, that means it's none of your fucking business. Got it?"

"Got it. Get out of my house," she yelled.

"Gladly." He turned and stalked toward the door and right out to his truck. He didn't look back. He heard the door slam when he was three feet away. He didn't care. He hopped in his truck, drove down the road, and gave himself some time to calm down. He wouldn't call Sid until a little bit later when he'd had a minute to chill. He didn't need to throw this stuff on Sid just yet. They'd maybe chat about it later, but not now.

29

H anna hummed as she refilled the bakery case to prepare for the morning rush. She looked up at the clock and saw that it was seven o'clock, time to open up.

Unlocking the front door, she went back into the kitchen to bring more cinnamon rolls out to the case. She carried out her tray of cinnamon rolls and smiled when her first customer walked in.

"Good morning, Jared. How are you? Want your cinnamon roll and coffee this morning?"

"I sure do, Hanna. Thank you."

She poured him a cup of coffee and slid that over on the counter.

He filled it with his fixings, which she knew by now was a lot of sugar and some creamer, as she pulled the cinnamon roll out of the case.

"You want it in a box to go?"

"Yeah, stick it in a box. I'm going to eat it in front of the guys at the job site."

She chuckled. "Well, that's kind of mean."

"I know, but they did that to me yesterday. I didn't have time to get in here. Did Dad tell you he's put me in charge of the barracks project?"

"He sure did. Congratulations. How's that going?"

"It's going all right. I mean, I'm learning the ropes, but I've been watching my dad for years, and he's the best of the best, so I think it's all going to be good. And I know he's right here if I have any questions."

Her heart expanded hearing Jared's pride in his dad. And she thought Quinn was pretty great, too, so... She chuckled. "That he is. He's very proud of you."

"Well, thank you. Happy to hear that. Anyway," he dropped his money on the counter and lifted his coffee and the cinnamon roll. "See you later."

"You bet. I'll see you later, Jared."

He left and a couple more customers entered. Her day had started out in bed with Quinn, which was pretty great, so she had every expectation the rest of it would be wonderful. Unless things went bad with Tisha.

Her mom showed up just after lunch. "Do you need help here today, hon?"

"I could use your help, Mom. Thank you. I have some loaves of bread rising. I need to get them in the oven. And I want to get the dough made up and ready to rise overnight for buns tomorrow."

"Okay, I can get that going."

Hanna cleaned up out front in the store. She wiped down the counter, rearranged the doughnut trays, so they didn't look so empty until she could refill them, and generally made it look presentable.

She put on a new pot of coffee and then walked back into the kitchen. Her mom was already busy working on the dough, but she couldn't resist asking her about Quinn.

"So, did you have a good night last night?"

Her cheeks turned instantly red. Of course, her mom didn't know the extent of how good her night was, but still, the embarrassment was there.

"Yes, I had a good night. Quinn liked meeting you and Dad. Thank you for being so gracious and caring to him. Not that I didn't expect that you would. I know what great hosts you are."

"Well, thank you, honey. And we're just so happy to see you with someone good. I've been asking around about him, and of course, he's been here forever, but boy, nobody has a bad word to say about him."

Hanna smiled. "Well, he's a pretty great guy. He runs a good, tight business. Keeps to himself. Has a tight circle of friends. And he's raised two great kids."

"That's what I hear."

Hanna went out front and emptied the garbage from behind the counter, and checked the kitchen garbage can. She pulled that bag out of the garbage can, too. "I'll be right back, Mama. I'm just going to throw this in the dumpster."

"Okay, honey."

She dragged the garbage bags out the back door, lifted the lid on the dumpster, and tossed her bags in.

Suddenly, someone grabbed her from behind. She struggled and squirmed and tried to kick back. Her hands clawed the hands around her mouth. Then she felt a rag covering her mouth and her nose.

Suddenly, her arms felt heavy. Her eyes felt heavy. Her legs felt heavy. She wasn't able to kick anymore. And then she didn't feel anything.

~

Hanna woke with a headache. She blinked, but her eyes were so dry, it felt like her eyelids were stuck to her eyeballs. Closing her eyes and rolling them around for a moment to moisten them, she tried again. It was dark wherever she was. She couldn't see anything. And the throbbing in her head was impossible to ignore.

Then she remembered that she was taking the garbage out and someone grabbed her. Her heartbeat increased and panic rose up her body.

She lifted her hands and found them to be tied in front of her, resting on her lap. She was sitting on what felt like a damp cement floor, propped up in a corner.

She struggled around. Her feet moved and weren't tied. That was good. She bent her knees and pushed herself up the wall with her shoulders.

"Don't. You. Move."

She froze. She didn't recognize the voice at all. She couldn't even tell if it was male or female.

"Wh...who are you?"

No answer.

"Please tell me who you are."

No answer.

She blinked a few times, hoping her eyes would adjust to the dimness of this room. Some shadows began to appear before her. But they were just that, shadows. She looked around to see if there was a window or a door. She saw a square on the far wall, but it was dark. Maybe a door or a boarded window. Her head pounded, and she tried clearing her head. "Please tell me who you are."

No sound. Suddenly, she heard movement from across the room. She froze. Was someone coming toward her? Whispers. There were two people here. Her breathing stilted as she felt the panic taking hold. They whispered a bit more, and it began to sound as if they argued.

"Find out."

"Give me some fucking time."

Heavy shuffling sounded across the room. Slow movements. And then she heard something thunk on the floor. Then a squeak. It sounded like somebody had moved a chair closer to her and sat on it.

She inhaled a breath and let it out slowly. Panicking would do no good now. She swallowed the lump in her throat and relaxed her shoulders. She needed to be strong.

When a voice finally spoke to her, it was slow and low. "I told you that you owed me money. And you little bitch, you are going to get it for me. Right now, I'm going to get that money from your rich boyfriend and your parents. They're going to pay us what that piece of shit husband of yours stole from us."

Oh, her heart hammered. Her throat dried up and a huge lump filled it. Oh my God. Oh my God. Oh my God. One of these crazy bitches got to her. Or two of them.

"I had nothing to do with Isaac's duplicity. I didn't know he was even doing that until somebody called me. I didn't even know that was a thing until somebody called me. Was it you who called me? You must have because you said you told me I owed you money."

"I don't care what you say. You were with him for a long time. You had to know what a piece of crap he was."

"Well, I did." She tried wetting her throat. "I mean, I didn't know he was doing this. We've been divorced for almost three years."

"Well, I don't care how long you've been divorced. He took money from me. And actually, I've done the checking. You were still married to him when he took money from me. Your divorce wasn't final yet when he took the first payment from me. That means you're complicit."

Her heart hammered in her chest. She tried to even out her ragged breathing, and she didn't even know what she could say to defend herself. This woman didn't want to listen to her at all.

"I had no idea he was doing this. I've been duped by him just as much as you have."

"Oh, really? Well, you know what he took from me? He took thirty-two thousand dollars from me. What did he take from you?"

She licked her lips. "Let's see. While we were married, he gambled away three cars, and I had to pay them off because we had loans on them even though he gambled them away. He almost gambled our house away. I've worked my tail off day and night to pay back his gambling debts so his fingers or legs wouldn't get broken by the thugs he gambled with. I was stupid to do it, but I did it. He's taken years of my life away from me. He's taken money away from me. He's taken a lot from me."

"Well, he took a lot from me, too. He took my dignity. He took my serenity. I can't trust anyone anymore because of him."

"Well, don't you think I feel the same way?"

"I don't care how you feel. Poor little you with your rich boyfriend. You can't trust anyone my ass. What I know is I want my money. That was my savings. That was for my retirement."

Her heart beat so hard it was painful. "I'm sorry that he did that, but I didn't have anything to do with it. Why don't you get an attorney and go after him?"

"Go after him for what? He doesn't have a job. He

doesn't have a house. He doesn't have anything. What the hell would I possibly get from him?"

"I don't know. Put him in jail. Make sure he can't ever do this to anybody again."

"Oh, we're going to make sure he doesn't do it to anybody again. But first, we're going to get our money back."

30

Quinn examined the stage at the Sandbar. "There's just a few more pieces to add to it and then it'll be completed," Brian bragged.

"It looks good, guys. You've done a great job. Thank you so much."

Jace strutted across the beach toward him.

Quinn turned and grinned at his friend. "What do you think of this?"

"I think it looks pretty fucking good. I can't wait till your party, Bud. What is that like two weeks away now?"

"Not even."

"Did you talk to Jami Hart?"

"I did. They're here and they're gonna play."

Jace clapped his hands together loudly. "Excellent. Excellent. It's gonna be fun. I've got the food ordered. I've got the booze ordered. I assume you're bringing a date."

"You know I am."

"Okay, good." Jace laughed. "Alright, I gotta get back in and get ready for the dinner crowd. What are you doing?"

"I'm gonna go pick up my girl and we are going to have dinner with Sid and Grace tonight."

"Yeah, I don't feel left out at all."

"You're welcome to join us, Bud. We're gonna be here, anyway. Hanna hasn't met Grace yet, and I wanted her to meet them since they're getting married soon, and I'm hoping Hanna will be in my life for a long time."

Jace grinned and slapped his buddy on the back. "Good for you, man. Good for you."

"So anyway, that's what I'm doing. I'll see you in a little while." He started toward his truck. "Actually, do we need to reserve a table?"

Jace laughed. "No, you can have this one right here, the one closest to the stage since no one seems to want it right now with the construction."

He chuckled. "Fine, we'll take it. It's a good view, anyway, don't you think?"

Jace looked up at the stage and grinned. "Man, it's great. I can't wait to start having concerts here. I'm gonna start calling bands and getting them set up."

"Excellent." Quinn's phone rang.

He didn't recognize the number, but he nodded to Jace. "Gotta take this, Bud. We'll see you later."

He started toward his truck as he answered his phone. "Quinn Kurtz."

"Quinn, it's Lance. Lance Valentine, Hanna's father. Hey, we can't find her. Is she with you?"

"No, I'm at the Sandbar finishing up a job here. What do you mean you can't find her? Isn't she at the bakery?"

"No, no. Allison was here helping Hanna. Hanna took the garbage out and she never came back. We're...Quinn, we're scared."

"I'll be right there." Quinn hung up the phone and ran

the rest of the way to his truck, got in, and sped to the bakery. His stomach tightened as he drove. Once he got to the bakery, Lance was waiting near the front door for him. He ran inside and shook Lance's hand.

"What's happening? Tell me what's going on."

Lance scraped his hand through his hair. "Allison's in the kitchen talking to the police. Hanna took the garbage out, and Allison was waiting for her to come back in. She never came back. So Allison went out to check and she couldn't find her anywhere. Her car's here. She's not answering her phone. We don't know where she's at. She wouldn't just leave. She's responsible. She has a business to run. She would have been back here. Where would she go without her purse and her car? Where would she go?"

"Okay. All right." Quinn scraped his hand through his hair and swallowed to keep his stomach from emptying its contents. This couldn't be happening. Things were going so well. Maybe too good, if there was such a thing.

"Okay. Let's go to the kitchen and talk to Allison."

"Yes, of course. Of course." Lance turned toward the kitchen, but he didn't look like the vibrant man he'd met yesterday. He looked older today. Worry etched lines in his face and his back rolled forward as if he'd aged twenty years overnight.

He followed Lance to the kitchen and found Allison sitting on a stool near the table. Two local police officers, Erin Moody and Trey Fielding, were standing in the kitchen asking her questions.

He shook both of their hands. "Hi, Erin. Trey."

"Hey, Quinn."

Allison looked up at him. "Oh, Quinn, please tell me you know where she is."

He shook his head slowly. "No, Allison, I'm sorry. I

don't. Can you please tell us all what happened? How long ago was this? When was the last time you saw her? Tell me everything."

Trey rested a hand on Quinn's shoulders. "Hey, Bud, let us ask the questions. Why don't you take a seat?"

Trey reached over and pulled another stool up next to the table. Quinn brushed it away. "I can't. I can't sit down." He swallowed again and glanced at Lance. "Why don't you sit, Lance?"

"I will. My knees are shaking."

Trey began to ask Allison questions. "When was the last time you saw her?"

"It was about an hour ago. She took the garbage out. She emptied the garbage from the front and the kitchen here and she took them out. She said, 'I'll be right back,' she never came back."

Trey responded. "Okay. So she doesn't have her purse and her car is still out there. And she didn't say anything about going to visit anybody. You didn't hear her talking to anyone outside."

"No, I didn't hear anything." Allison began to weep, and Lance put his arm around her shoulders.

"Okay," Trey said. "Erin is going to go check with the local businesses and see if anybody has cameras that maybe recorded someone with Hanna. And we'll see what we can find there. I'm going to go out and peruse the area and see if I can find any evidence of anything. And she's not answering her phone, you said."

Erin stepped out the back door and Quinn swallowed the hot lump that had formed in his throat.

Allison managed to say, "I've been calling her and calling her and calling her and she's not answering her phone."

Quinn pulled his phone out and tapped Hanna's number. The phone rang and rang. She didn't answer. He closed his eyes and lifted his face to the ceiling. "Fuck."

Trey turned. "What?"

She was getting prank calls last night, so I asked her if she minded turning her phone off so we could finish dinner without the interruption, and I'll bet she never turned it back on."

Trey nodded. "Okay. Well, that means we won't be able to track her with her phone. We'll try though. Text me her number."

He and Trey had been friends for a number of years. At this time, Quinn was happy to know he was on this case. He was a great cop. Quinn texted Hanna's phone number to Trey. His fingers shook. His stomach quelled. His shoulders began to stiffen.

Trey looked at him. "Quinn, do you know anyone who would want to cause her harm? Who was prank calling her?"

"Isaac called her last night."

"Who is Isaac?"

"Her ex-husband. He said he was in town and wanted to talk to her and she refused to see him."

"Okay. Do you know where he's staying?"

"I don't know anything about him other than he's a deadbeat, and he's a criminal."

Quinn turned to Lance. "Do you know where he might be staying?"

Lance slowly shook his head. "Nope. We don't know anything about where he is. He hasn't made any contact with us, and he wouldn't. He knows we didn't think much of him. And you're right. He's a criminal." Lance ran his hand down his face. "But he wouldn't kidnap her. I mean, I don't think he would kidnap her."

"All right. So Isaac, who else?"

Quinn sucked in a deep breath and let it out in a whoosh. "Tisha."

Trey's eyebrow shot up into his hairline. "Seriously?"

"She followed us home last night from Lance and Allison's house. I did go see her this morning. I don't think she would do anything to Hanna. I honestly don't. She's manipulative, and she's deceitful. And last night, she wasn't thinking straight. But I don't think she has it in her to kidnap anyone or bring harm to anyone other than in a manipulative sort of way."

"All right. Tisha. Who else?"

"Well, there's three women who have been calling Hanna wanting money because Isaac catfished them."

Trey stopped writing and turned to look at him. "This guy really is a piece of shit."

"He is."

"So he catfished these women."

Quinn nodded. "I guess he took a lot of money from them, as in thousands. Twenty thousand, thirty thousand dollars. And they were calling Hanna, wanting her to pay them back because she had been married to him at one point."

"Well, okay." He wrote in his notebook. "Who else knows about this?"

Lance responded. "Grant Park, my attorney."

"Okay." Trey wrote Grant's name down.

"We went to him and asked him what we could do, and he said if those women called to have them call his office. I don't know if anyone has. I know Hanna did get one more phone call and told her to call Grant. So you could check with him."

"I'll do that." Trey kept writing.

When he was finished writing, he said, "Anything else that you can think of."

Quinn felt like he was going to throw up. He leaned against the stainless-steel table, took a deep breath, and shook his head slowly. "No. Nothing I can think of. Have you checked with Jalyn, her friend?"

"Nope. We'll check with her. Last I saw her she was riding out of town on a fire truck though."

"Yeah." He nodded and wished he had Jalyn's phone number.

"Okay. So we're going to do some investigating. We're going to look around outside. Please don't go near the dumpster until we've gathered any evidence there might be. If you can think of anyone else who may want to cause her harm, let us know."

Quinn nodded and stared at her parents. Both of them looked about as sick as he felt.

Trey started toward the back door, but it opened and Erin stepped inside. "There are tire tracks in the parking area next to Hanna's car. They lead out of the alley. The mud from the alley transferred to the road for a few feet, but it appears the vehicle flew out onto the square in the wrong direction."

Quinn stepped into the back hall near the back door. "Any idea what kind of vehicle?"

Erin locked eyes with him. "Small tread pattern. I'm thinking a Prius. Lucky for us they ran through the potholes and left nice prints. That also left the pattern on the road showing they went in the wrong direction."

The front door to the bakery opened and Allison began to slide off her stool. "Oh, the door is unlocked."

Quinn shook his head. "I've got it, Allison."

He hurried out front and saw his son, Jared, standing at the counter.

"Hey, Jared, what are you doing here?"

"I came to get a sandwich and a cinnamon roll."

"Oh." Quinn took a deep breath. "Hanna's missing, Jared. We're trying to find her."

Jared slid the baseball cap off and scratched the top of his head. "Is there anything I can do?"

"Have you noticed anything recently around here? We're thinking about an hour ago is when she was taken. And we're thinking it was someone in a smaller vehicle, like a Prius."

Jared shrugged. "Not many of those around here."

Quinn froze. "We saw them at the barracks last week."

"We did, Dad. I saw some there today that looked fresh. I thought those kids were back and saw our stuff there and left."

"Hang on." Quinn hustled to the kitchen where Lance and Allison were. "I have to go. Stay close to your phones."

He hustled toward the back door. "Trey. Erin. I have a lead. The barracks. We've seen Prius tire tracks there the past week and Jared said he saw fresh ones there today."

Trey looked at Erin. "You stay and finish the investigation here, so we don't lose any evidence. I'll go with Quinn."

They hustled through the bakery. Quinn stopped in the kitchen. "You may want to lock the front door behind us."

Lance stood and shuffled toward him. He didn't wait.

He hurried through the bakery, collected Jared, and ran to his truck. Jared jumped in with him. Trey was already in his cruiser and rushing the wrong way out of the square toward the barracks.

31

Hanna pleaded with this woman, these women, whoever they were. "Please know if I had the money I would help you hire an attorney."

"We don't need your help to hire an attorney. We want our money back. That was part of my retirement, hers, too. I gave it to that piece of shit because he was going to come and marry me. He said he was going to. He said he loved me."

The other woman spoke for the first time. Her footsteps drew near, her voice was softer. "He said he was going to marry me, too. Told me he wanted to start a business, and we'd work it together."

Hanna felt bad for these women, but she was also afraid of them. "Have you ever met him in person?"

The first woman barked, "No, I never did. He said you kept stealing the money. I would send him money to come to me, and he said you got a hold of it and stole it. You have all my money."

Hanna shook her head and was immediately sorry as the headache slammed hard. "I didn't steal anything from him. It was quite the opposite. He's been stealing from me. As a matter of fact, I couldn't even afford to buy a thirty-five-dollar bathroom vanity at a thrift store because he had cleared out my bank account just two weeks ago."

"We don't want your pity story. He said you were stealing from him."

Hanna threw caution to the wind. "He also said he was going to come and marry you."

The woman yelled, "Quiet! I don't want to hear anything from you. Do you understand me? You're liars. You're both liars."

Hanna's stomach twisted. Her breathing came in spurts and she consciously tried to slow her breathing down, so panic didn't cloud her judgment. But she was getting closer to panic with each passing minute.

"I'm not a liar. I'm not a liar." She repeated. "I was duped by him just like you were."

"I don't want to hear it." The first woman barked again.

Hanna tried a softer tactic. "Have you tried getting in touch with him?"

"How would I get in touch with him? The only way I was able to get in touch with him was from a cell phone that he gave me that he no longer answers."

Hanna swallowed. That's how he was doing it. He had different cell phones. Likely pre-paids.

She inhaled a deep breath. "He called me last night. He said he was in town and wanted to meet. I told him no."

The second woman came closer. "He said he wanted to meet you and he's in town. Where is he in town?"

She swallowed. "I have no idea. I didn't want to meet him. I told him no."

The first woman asked, "Are you sure he's in town?"

Hanna shrugged. She wished she could see these women. If she could look into their eyes, they'd hopefully see she was being truthful with them. "Well, he asked me to come and meet him and I said no."

The second woman, with the softer voice, asked, "Where would he be then? Does he have friends here?"

Hanna scoffed. "No, he doesn't have friends. If he'd be anywhere, he'd be at the hotel."

The first woman jumped up quickly, knocking the chair over, and stormed toward the door. Hanna watched the door open and light filled the room. One woman was muscular with short, spiked hair. The other woman had longer hair, just past her shoulders. It was blonde, and she was on the small side. She heard the door lock from the outside and swallowed the despair climbing up her spine. She'd get out of here. If they didn't find Isaac, what would they do to her? So far, they hadn't hurt her, and she was their bargaining chip. That made her feel better.

She'd been sitting for a while. Stiffness had settled in, but she leaned forward on her hands, which were bound together with what felt like zip ties. She managed to stand. Taking a deep breath, she inched along the wall closest to the door.

Because she couldn't really see anything anymore, she brushed her back along the wall as she made her way. Slowly hugging the wall, her hands in front of her. As soon as she reached the door, she nearly wept.

She tried turning the knob, and it turned, but the door wouldn't budge. She started kicking the door. Pounding with her fists, hoping anyone would hear. She exhausted herself and leaned with her back against the door. She glanced around the room and remembered the big dark spot on the wall on the other side of the room. She slid along the walls toward the other side until she felt the frame of a window. It was covered with a board.

Using the zip ties between her wrists, she tried catching the zip tie under the corner of the board and pulling it away. The searing pain that shot through her as the zip ties cut into her wrists was nothing compared to the fear of what these women would do to her if they didn't find Isaac.

She kept pulling and tugging and scratching against the board. Finally, the zip ties between her wrists broke.

She sobbed as tingling raced up her arms. The warm stickiness of blood on her wrists made her nauseous. She let her arms hang for a moment and then remembered the chair across the room.

She crawled on the floor until she found the over-turned chair. She picked it up and dragged it across the room. Once she was near the window again, she lifted the chair and beat it against the board and the window.

Bang. Bang. Bang. Bang.

Another little piece of the corner of the board broke off and a little light shone through. She stuck the leg of the chair into the hole she made and tried using it to pry the board apart. She broke a little more of the board away and was encouraged to continue beating at it and prying it apart.

She kept working at the board until she had enough broken away that she felt she could probably crawl out.

Taking the leg of the chair, she scraped it along the window's ledge to make sure there was no pointed glass that would cut into her.

She squeezed her head through the opening only to see she was on the third floor. Tears flooded her eyes as her heart sank.

Allowing herself a bit of a pity party, she sucked in a deep breath and decided she was going to get the fuck out of there! With her fingers, she pulled and tugged on that board, breaking more of it away from the window.

And when she had enough, she began screaming out of the window. She screamed as loud as she'd ever screamed in her life.

And finally someone hollered up to her, "Hanna!"

She looked down only to see someone run around the corner of the building. She sobbed. Someone heard her and knew it was her. She slowly moved toward the door. Someone was coming!

The second they pulled into the barracks parking lot, Quinn's eyes scanned the area for the tracks. He saw them right away.

"There they are." He pointed.

Jared nodded. "There's more over there."

He followed the tracks with his truck, careful not to run over them in case the police needed pictures or to take impressions.

He stopped in front of the third building and hopped from his truck, his eyes scanning the ground for other tracks. He found two sets of footprints, a smaller set of prints looked to be walking backward.

Trey pulled to a stop at the far end of the building, his head down as he walked toward them, looking at the tracks. Jared ran to the door and noticed it was unlocked.

"Dad. Someone left this door open."

He stepped near his son, careful to straddle the footprints. Thank goodness it had rained last night. The tracks were easy to follow.

Banging sounded from the back of the building. Bang. Bang.

Jared said, "I'll go see what that is, Dad."

Jared ran around the building and Quinn continued inside. He heard Jared yell, "Hanna."

He froze. As he turned to see if Hanna was outside, Jared ran into the building.

"Dad, it's Hanna. She's on the third floor."

He took the steps two at a time and lengthened his stride beyond where he should have. He wasn't letting age stop him today. He was getting Hanna.

As they landed on the third floor, he and Jared began opening the doors of each of the individual rooms and calling for Hanna.

Toward the middle of the hallway, one door had a new swivel staple safety lock installed. A padlock secured the door.

He grabbed the lock and tugged on it. "Hanna, are you in there?"

He beat on the door. "Hanna,"

She yelled, "Quinn, Quinn, I'm in here. I'm in here. Can you help me?"

She pounded on the door from inside.

Jared said, "I'll run to the building and get something to cut the lock."

Quinn shook his head. "Never mind. I'm busting the door down." He stepped back slightly and yelled. "Hanna, stand back."

He and Jared both kicked at the door near the lock. The wood on the door began to splinter, especially around where the safety swivel latch had been installed. Jared lifted his leg higher and kicked the door next to the latch. Trey reached the third floor and stood nearby as they kicked the door.

The wood cracked loudly and began to break away from the lock. A few more well-placed kicks and the lock broke away from the door. Quinn twisted the doorknob and pushed the door open.

Hanna ran into his arms.

His heart beat so hard and his eyes welled with tears the instant he held her. His arms wrapped tightly around her as she sobbed into his chest.

After a few moments, he whispered, "Let's get you out of here."

"Yes," she hiccupped. She lifted her hands to wipe her tears. That's when he saw the blood on her wrists and hands.

He felt a rage like he'd never felt before. "Honey, you're hurt?"

"I want to get out of here. I want to get out of here. Please take me out of here before they come back."

Trey entered the room and looked around with his flashlight.

Quinn stared into her beautiful blue eyes. "Who are they?"

"Those women. Those women that Isaac catfished. That's who it is. They had me."

"Where are they now, honey?"

"They went to see if he's at the hotel. I don't know what they're going to do to him. They were going to blackmail you to get their money back in exchange for me."

"OK. Well, they're not going to do that now."

She stepped back slightly and took a deep breath. She swallowed and turned to see Jared breathing heavily, watching her closely. "Thank you, Jared."

Quinn watched as his nostrils flared and he took a deep breath. He was proud of his boy. So damned proud.

Focusing on Hanna once more, he asked, "Can you walk, honey?"

"Yes. Yes, I can walk."

They took a couple of steps and she moved slowly and surely. He bent down and picked her up. "Well, I don't care."

"Quinn, I can walk."

"I know. Just let me do this."

He carried her to the staircase. Jared ran ahead of them, opening doors wherever they were needed at each level.

As soon as he got her to the first floor, he moved immediately to the main door and outside.

Erin ran toward them. "Are you okay, Hanna? My name is Erin Moody. I'm a police officer here in Blossom Springs."

"I'm fine. I'm fine now. Those women, they went to the hotel to see if they could find Isaac. He stole money from them, and they want it back. That's who took me."

"Ok." Erin glanced his way, "Is Trey upstairs?"

"Yes," he called over his shoulder. "I'm taking her to the hospital."

"We'll be there shortly. Go ahead."

Jared opened the back door to the truck, as Quinn gently set Hanna inside.

Jared said, "Dad, go ahead and sit with her. I'll drive."

He didn't need to be told twice. He hopped in the back seat next to Hanna, wrapped her in his arms, and they took off toward the hospital.

He picked up her hands and looked at her wrists. The zip ties were still wrapped around her wrists, but you could see where the one tying her two wrists together had broken. These had cut deeply into her wrists.

"We'll get these cleaned up, honey. Doctors will take care of you, and make sure there's no infection."

She didn't say anything. She simply lay her head on Quinn's shoulder.

He kissed the top of her head, and he held her hand. "Jared, call Lance and Allison and tell them we have her. The last call I received was from Lance. Just tap that number on the screen."

"Okay."

The phone came through the speakers, the ringing ended, and Lance answered, "Hello."

"Lance, it's Quinn. We have her. She's fine. We're taking her to the hospital. Meet us there."

Lance said to Allison. "Mama, they have her."

Allison could be heard sobbing, and Lance said, "We have to go see her."

Lance said into the phone, "I'm sorry, Quinn. Can we talk to her?"

Hanna swallowed and sat up a bit straighter. "I'm alright, Daddy. I can't wait to see you."

Allison sobbed again, and Lance said, "I'm hanging up. We'll be there soon."

The call ended, and Quinn grinned. He couldn't express how happy he was it ended as it did. He laid his cheek on top of her head as she once again leaned against him. "I will never let anything happen to you again. I promise. I promise we're going to get those women, and then I'm going to do everything in my power to make sure you're always safe."

He heard her sob gently, and he squeezed her a little

tighter. They sat quietly together until Jared pulled them into the hospital parking lot.

He slid out of the truck first, then reached in, picked her up, and began carrying her into the hospital. "Quinn, please let me walk."

"I want to help you."

"Then let me walk. I'm capable."

He frowned but gently set her feet on the ground. He walked alongside her with his arm around her shoulders, Jared at his side.

As soon as they entered the hospital, a whirlwind of things happened. Hanna didn't have her purse and no insurance information. Questions were asked. A million questions. He was beginning to lose his temper and finally snapped. "Can't you help her first by cutting those zip ties from her wrists and making sure she doesn't need any other medical care? If you're worried about the money, I'll cover it. Just help her."

The nurses all stopped and stared. Finally, an older lady came forward with a wheelchair. "Honey, take a seat and let me get you back to an exam room."

His heart beat rapidly, and he inhaled a deep breath and let it out slowly. He looked at the clerk he'd snapped at and said, "I apologize. I shouldn't have lost my temper."

She smiled sweetly. "Thank you. I understand your worry and frustration. I often think it's worse up here checking in than anything that goes on back there."

He nodded. "Thank you for understanding." He glanced at Jared and cocked his head. "Let's go sit with Hanna."

H anna watched the doctor work on her wrists, cleaning them out and making sure the zip ties didn't shred or pieces weren't embedded into her skin. A nurse stood nearby, her name tag said Monique, typing into a computer when the doctor said anything.

She winced a few times as the doctor pulled gently on her wounds or touched a sore spot. At least sorer than the others. Now that the adrenaline was wearing off, her wrists were tender. She saw Quinn's jaw tighten when she winced. It made her heart swell that he cared so much. He'd sent Jared to the job site to explain what happened and to be there and oversee the work being done. Jared seemed relieved not to have to sit here. He smiled at her before he left and quietly said, "I'm glad you're alright, Hanna."

She smiled in return. "Thanks to you and your dad."

His cheeks reddened, and she thought it was cute. Someday she'd have to ask Quinn to see a picture of him at twenty-five years of age. She'd bet he looked remarkably like Jared looked right now.

As soon as Jared left, her parents came bustling into the room. "Oh my God. Oh, praise the Lord my baby is alright." Her mom wailed.

The doctor stepped back a moment. "You all go ahead and have your greeting, then I'll finish."

Her mom hugged her. Then her dad slowly approached. His eyes glistened with unshed tears and his cheeks were red. He slowly leaned down and hugged her. "I'm so happy you're still with us Hanna. I love you so much it hurts, and I couldn't bear it if you weren't in my life anymore."

"I love you too, Daddy. So much."

He stepped back and sniffed. He pulled a hanky from his pocket and swiped his nose, refolding his hanky and tucking it into his back pocket. He moved over to Quinn, who stood and hugged her dad. He then asked him to sit in the seat he'd just vacated. Tears welled in her eyes, witnessing it all.

The doctor stepped forward once more. "May I continue?"

She mustered a smile. "Yes. Please."

Her mom dutifully sat in the second chair in the room but craned her neck to see everything the doctor did. He shined an ultraviolet light on her wounds. "This will show me any pieces of plastic that may have broken off."

Hanna nodded and watched as he slowly moved the light around her wrist. He found one small piece and used a tweezer to remove it, which pinched slightly. She winced and pinched her lips together. Maybe she shouldn't watch what he did.

As soon as he was confident he'd gotten everything out, he stood. "Monique will clean you up, apply antibacterial ointment, and wrap your wrists. I'd like to see you in my office in three or four days, as the swelling goes down, to make sure I didn't miss anything. Right now, you're swollen and that could be hiding some minute threads of plastic."

"Thank you," she offered. He nodded to her parents and shook Quinn's hand. He exited the room and Monique efficiently slid a tray on wheels next to her bed, sat on the stool the doctor just vacated, and gently began dabbing at the dried blood on her wrists.

"How's your headache, Hanna?" Monique inquired.

"It's better, thank you."

"Whatever they used to render you unconscious is what gave you the headache. You don't have any lumps on your head. We only gave you something for that. If it comes back, take something you're used to taking for headaches. But hopefully, once you've eaten and rested, you'll be fine."

Just as Monique mentioned food, her stomach growled. She hadn't even thought about being hungry.

Quinn chuckled.

"I guess I'm a little hungry. What time is it?"

He leaned forward. "It's six-thirty."

"Oh no! We were supposed to have dinner with Sid and Grace."

He nodded. "They understand you're indisposed and we're to call them when you're up to it. And they're getting married in two weeks. So, hopefully we'll get to dine with them before then, but if not, when they get home from their honeymoon."

"I'm fine other than having two new bracelets." She

held up the wrist Monique had finished bandaging and Quinn's lips tightened slightly, but he tried smiling.

"When you're ready, you just let me know and we'll see what their schedule is like."

Hanna's mom fussed a little bit. "We have leftovers at home. Why don't you stop by the house to have something to eat? I'm sorry I didn't have time to make anything else."

She shook her head. "Don't worry about it, Mom. It's alright. I think I have something at home."

Quinn stood neared the bed. "I think you should come and stay with me. Your house is a construction zone and I have a big house all to myself. I'll take good care of you, I promise."

Her mom tittered a bit, and Hanna almost rolled her eyes. "Oh, honey, that sounds really nice. Quinn, you are such a sweet man."

Hanna's lips turned up in a smile and her eyes locked on Quinn's. His cheeks turned pink. He smiled. "See, your mom thinks it's a good idea."

There wasn't much to think about. Of course, she'd stay with Quinn. It would give them some time to really get to know each other.

Trey and Erin entered the room as Monique finished up the second wrist. They shook Quinn's hand, then her mom and dad's.

Erin stepped forward. "How are you, Hanna?"

"I'm good. My wrists are cut up from using the zip ties from trying to escape. My headache is gone and I have everyone around me."

"Good to hear. We have the women and Isaac in custody. They had gotten ahold of him at the hotel and they beat on him pretty good. We had to separate them at the jail because those women are hot mad."

Hanna smiled. "Isaac deserves to be beat on. I wanted to do it so many times and never had the guts."

Her father said. "I wanted to beat on him, too."

Her mom turned and stared at her father as if he'd grown a second head. Her dad shrugged. "What?"

Her mom shook her head and turned her attention back to Erin. "What happens now?"

Erin smiled. "They'll need to make bail. The DA is working on the charges right now. Kidnapping, bodily injury, and breaking and entering to name just a few of the charges. There will likely be others coming too. As for Isaac, catfishing is not explicitly a crime, unfortunately. But he took money under false pretenses, and the women want their money back. They're pressing charges against him for a variety of things. As soon as they calm down and actually hire an attorney, we'll see what charges come to him. The DA is also working with them on their charges against him. He's working with the DAs in their respective cities because moving money across state lines under false pretenses can be criminal. That'll be up to them, though. For now, we wanted you to know you're safe. They are locked up."

Hanna smiled. "Thank you. I do feel better knowing they are locked up."

Trey nodded. "If it's any consolation, they are both sorry for kidnapping you. They let their rage and hurt cloud their logic. After they've had some time to calm down and get some rest, I think they'll be very embarrassed and sorry. That won't change the charges, though. And I think we can all agree, it was a good thing they hadn't thought this through very well. They weren't organized and prepared for...well, anything. In the police business, we like amateur criminals. They're easy to catch."

Hanna chuckled. "Thank you."

They said their goodbyes and left, and Monique announced that she could be released. "I do hate to tell you, though. You do have to take care of things at the front desk." She glanced at Quinn who turned beet red.

"I'm sorry about my outburst."

Monique shrugged. "It's fine. We all know emotions were high."

Hanna turned to look at her mom. "I don't have my purse, Mom."

"I have it in the car, honey."

Quinn stood and held his hand out. "If you give me your keys, Allison, I'll go to your car and get Hanna's purse."

Her mom tittered again, and her dad shook his head as he stood. He pulled keys from his pocket and handed them to Quinn. "Thank you, son."

Quinn's eyes shot to hers and she smiled at him. That meant a lot to him right there.

Quinn and Hanna sat in the Florida Room at his house. Her bandages were now off, and while her wrists were red and scabbed over, she looked as beautiful as ever.

They had been having their morning coffee out here on the sectional, looking out over the fields and watching the horses graze. His phone chimed a text, and he pulled it from his pocket.

"How about dinner tonight?" Sid.

"Sid wants to have dinner tonight. How do you feel about that?"

"I'd love it."

He replied to Sid. "Tonight is good. Six?"

He got a thumbs-up in reply.

He resumed his position of sitting next to Hanna with his arm around her shoulders as they enjoyed the serenity of the day.

She sighed. "It really is beautiful out here."

"It is. That's why I built here. I've never been as at peace though, as I have since you've been here."

She tilted her face up to his. "Aww, that's really sweet of you."

He chuckled. "Why don't you move in?"

Her brows shot up. "Really? Isn't it soon?"

"Well, maybe for some. But we're not teenagers. We've been through an awful lot, and I know in my heart, I want to be with you forever Hanna Valentine."

She sat forward and turned to face him. The blue of her eyes was his new favorite color. He brushed her cheek with the back of his fingers softly and grinned. "I love you, Hanna Valentine."

She swallowed. "I love you too, Quinn Kurtz."

"Do you want to move in with me?"

She finally smiled. "My mom will be over the moon."

"As nice as that is, what about you? Will you be over the moon?"

She took in a deep breath, set her coffee cup on the little table in front of the sectional, and took his hand in hers.

"I will be over the moon. I already am. I've never felt more loved or protected or cared for than I have in the time we've been together, which is really only about a month."

"Why does the time matter so much to you?"

She swallowed. "I just don't want us to be caught up in the moments of these peaceful mornings and forget that I leave my shoes too close to the door sometimes. Or you leave your dirty underwear on the bathroom floor. That we'll have things that we disagree on and we both have businesses to run."

He leaned forward and kissed her lips softly. "Are you saying you won't move in because I leave my underwear on the bathroom floor?"

"No." She took a deep breath. "Quinn." She swallowed. "I have honestly never loved anyone like I love you. That's stupid to say because I was married. But it was never like this." She motioned between them. "I now know my relationship with Isaac felt more like a duty and a chore because I made the decision to marry him and I didn't want to be wrong. So I tolerated too much."

He sat for a moment, staring into her eyes. His heart felt close to bursting. "Okay. I'll pick up my underwear if it's that important."

She laughed. At first it was a small laugh. Then she laughed a bit harder.

He sat forward and took her hands in his. "I understand it's scary. It is for me, too. I didn't have an easy first marriage. But, sweetheart, it was never like this. I never called her sweetheart. I never wanted to spend mornings with her, doing nothing and talking. It was a duty for me in ways, too. This isn't. When you were kidnapped, all I could think was I didn't want to live my life without you in it."

He slid down to the floor, with one knee down, her soft hands in his, her eyes beginning to well with tears. "Hanna Valentine. Will you marry me?"

She swallowed and sniffed lightly. "I certainly will."

He kissed her lips. Pushing himself up onto the sectional, he lay over her soft, pliable body, holding himself up on his elbows. His hands cradled her head as he stared at her. "I love you, Hanna."

She giggled. "I love you, too."

He kissed her lips fully. Her arms wrapped around his body and pulled him close. He'd honestly never felt so loved in his life. And he'd never felt so ready to offer unconditional love before. Other than his kids. But he was all in, one thousand percent.

He lifted himself up and pulled her up to a standing position. "We have to go."

"Go where?" Her pretty brows pushed together.

"Buy a ring."

"Quinn, it's only seven o'clock, and it's Saturday."

"Yes. I'm aware."

"And your party is tonight."

"Also aware."

"We have things we have to do today. Like, decorate the Sandbar."

"We don't have to do that until later, and I want you to do it with my ring on your finger."

"It won't make us more engaged."

"Right. But everyone will see it. And I want everyone to know you're mine and we're getting married."

"What about Jared and Jenny? Shouldn't you tell them first?"

"I told them yesterday."

She shook her head quickly. "What?"

"I've been thinking about this since you came home with me from the hospital. Every day for the past two weeks, I've known more and more I wanted you to always be here. Yesterday I told them. They're happy, by the way."

"I haven't even met Jenny."

"I know. She's coming home next weekend to meet you. And..." He took her left hand in his and tapped her ring finger. "I want you to have a ring on this finger right here."

She inhaled deeply, then let it out. She stared into his eyes for a long time. The entire time, his heart was beating rapidly. "Okay. Let's go pick out rings."

"Rings as in plural?"

"Well, you are going to wear a wedding ring, Mr. Kurtz, so we need to pick out matching rings."

He laughed and pulled her through the house. "Now you're talking."

EPILOGUE

Hanna pulled the hot curling iron out of a curl she'd meticulously wound around the hot iron and watched it fall. Taking another chunk of hair, she did it again, only this time, she watched the sparkles shoot off her engagement ring in the mirror. Her lips turned up in a smile so big the skin on her face stretched. She loved looking at her ring.

Quinn stepped into the bathroom and leaned against the door jamb. "You're going to outshine the bride."

Laughing, she pulled the curling iron out of this curl and turned to him. "Doubtful. Grace is gorgeous. She'll no doubt be especially gorgeous today."

Pushing off the doorjamb with his shoulder, he came to stand behind her. His hands slid around her waist and pulled her body back into his. She set the hot iron on the counter and lay her hands over his, enjoying the sparkler on her left hand. His lips dipped near her ear. "I love seeing you wear my ring."

She chuckled. "I was just thinking how much I love looking at it and wearing it."

He kissed her ear and squeezed her before stepping back. "How much longer before you're ready?"

"Give me five minutes. I want to pull my hair up so it isn't so hot. Then I'll step into my dress."

"I can help with that."

"No, you can't." She laughed. "You can help me out of it tonight, though."

"I'm all over that."

She stared at him a moment. "You look great in white pants and the tropical print shirt. That was clever of Grace and Sid to think of them."

He turned with his arms out so she could see the full effect. "It's cooler too."

"I'll bet."

He winked and left the room. She wrapped two more locks of hair around the hot iron, then swept her hair back and twisted it into a French twist, but let the long ends spring from the top. She pinned her twist into place, then let the long curls drape over it. Spraying her bangs in place, she swiped on her lip gloss and stepped back.

She slipped on a purple sundress that matched the purple in Quinn's tropical print shirt. That was Grace's idea. She appreciated being accepted by Grace and Sid, and that Grace made sure she felt included. They'd become good friends to her.

She left the bathroom, flicking off the light on her way past the switch, and found Quinn sitting on the sofa, chatting on the phone. He didn't look relaxed. In fact, he was leaning forward and looked about ready to jump.

He turned his head and saw her watching him. Inhaling a deep breath, he pulled the phone away from his ear and handed it to her. "Tisha called to see if I minded that she speak with you. I told her I didn't mind, exactly like I told her before. However, here we are. Do you want to speak with her?"

Hanna took a deep breath and reached for the phone. Their fingers brushed when she took the phone, and she made sure to stay right where she was so he could hear.

Tapping the speaker icon, she stared at Quinn while she spoke to Tisha.

"Hi, Tisha. How are you?"

"I'm fine. Thank you for asking. I'm sorry I didn't call sooner, but I wanted to give you time to heal."

"I'm healed. Thank you for the time, though."

"I just wanted to tell you I'm sorry for following you from your parents' home. It was wrong and I don't want you to feel like I'd ever cause you harm. And congratulations on your engagement. Quinn is a lucky man. I truly mean that."

She looked into Quinn's eyes as he listened to his ex-wife on the phone. Responding to Tisha, she smiled at Quinn. "Actually, I think I'm the lucky one. But thank you. From both of us."

"Okay. Well, I know you're getting ready for Sid and Grace's wedding, so I won't keep you."

"Thank you for understanding Tisha. Do you mind if I ask you a question?"

Tisha hesitated slightly. "No, not at all."

"When you told me a few weeks ago that you felt like someone was following you, were you being honest with me?"

Tisha sighed heavily and cleared her throat. "No. I had followed you that day, and it was my feeble attempt to make you feel paranoid. I should never have done that. I guess I was jealous. I apologize for doing that. Please forgive me."

Quinn's brows shot up. Hanna swallowed and took a breath. She tamped down the irritation that rose up. Because what would it serve to snap at Tisha now? She'd called to apologize, and she'd admitted what she did. "I forgive you. But, as we move forward, I ask two things of you. One, you never do anything like that again. And two, the kids are never to be put in the middle of anything between the three of us. The three of us meaning, Quinn, yourself, and me."

"I give my word that I'll never do that again or anything similar to harm you in any way and I won't put the kids in a situation where they are the go-betweens or in the middle of anything that pertains to us."

"Thank you, Tisha. I'd like us to get along and be friends even. It makes things so much easier as our family grows. Once the kids marry and have babies, we'll be seeing each other, and it should be comfortable for everyone."

"I agree. Thank you for being so mature about all of this, Hanna. I do admire you and think of you as a friend. I'd also like to let you know that I started working for my father last week. It's only an office position, but since I need a job, I'm happy for it."

Quinn grinned and winked at her and Hanna's tummy filled with flutters. "I think of you as a friend too, Tisha. Thank you. And congratulations on your job. I wish you all the best with it."

"Thank you. It's certainly a change and I know I should have done this a long time ago, but..."

Hanna grinned at Quinn. "At least you have it now. I

hate to cut this short, but we do have to leave. I'll talk to you later."

"Yes. Have a great time today. Goodbye, Hanna."

The call ended, and she handed Quinn his phone. He stood and pocketed it into his front pants pocket. The style today was for the heat spell they'd been having. Sid and Grace opted to get married on the stage at the Sandbar. The theme was shoes optional. They were as down-to-earth as two folks could be.

Quinn held his hand out to her, and she eagerly took it, squeezing his fingers. They left their house and drove to the Sandbar for the wedding ceremony of one of Quinn's oldest friends. Grace's brother, Travis Murphy, would give her away. Quinn and Jace stood as the witnesses and Grace's niece was the third witness. That was all they wanted.

After arriving at the Sandbar, Grace rushed to her and took Hanna's hands in hers. "I have a huge favor to ask of you, Hanna."

"Of course, whatever I can do."

"Will you stand with me as my bridesmaid and witness? My niece broke her foot playing soccer last night and can't be here."

Hanna's heart swelled. "Really? You want me?"

"I do. I believe it's not only the start of Sid and I's marriage, but the beginning of a lifelong friendship between us. I'd love it if you'd honor me and stand with me."

"I'd be the one who is honored, and yes, I'm happy to stand with you and be a witness."

Grace kissed her cheek and pulled her to the back of the Sandbar where her bouquet of flowers lay on a table with Grace's pretty white roses and sunflowers. Her bouquet was sunflowers and lavender, and it was stunning.

Grace handed her the bouquet. "It's almost like this was meant to be. It matches what you're wearing perfectly."

Hanna laughed. "It actually does."

They moved through pictures and instructions from the minister. Quinn, Sid, and Jace entered the Sandbar after having had photos taken outside, and she was granted the honor of pinning Quinn's boutonniere on. The white rose was perfect on his shirt.

Sid cleared his throat. "Let's go get us married now."

The five of them walked together to the stage outside. Quinn held his arm out for her to hold as they ascended the steps to the top of the stage. He stopped and kissed her softly before stepping a few steps over to allow room for Sid and Grace between them.

Jace and Sid came up the other steps and stood next to Quinn. Finally, Grace was escorted across the beach by her brother, Travis, and came to stand between Sid and her.

The minister started the ceremony. A few of the townspeople were invited to the ceremony. They wanted to keep it small. Sitting front and center was Coop, the older gentleman Sid purchased the garage from, and his wife. She recognized a few people, and her parents and Jalyn were there as well. Jared and Jenny were watching, both of them smiling brightly. She felt so proud to be here with this group of people and as her thoughts turned to her own wedding; she glanced over and saw Quinn watching her instead of Sid and Grace saying their vows. He winked at her and the smile that floated across her face was instant. Butterflies flew in her belly, and she once again thought how lucky she was to have him in her life.

Her parents were over the moon happy about their engagement. Isaac, well he'd somehow managed to bail himself out of jail and had taken off for parts unknown. Quinn had a brief conversation with Isaac just before he'd been released. He wouldn't tell her what he said to Isaac, only that she'd never hear from him again. She was more than fine with that.

Epilogue - Quinn

Quinn tucked his fingers under the little purple straps that held Hanna's sundress on her body. He'd thought of this all day. Every time he looked at her, he was once again smitten with her beauty. She was incredible. But as he introduced her to the townspeople who came to celebrate Sid and Grace and listen to Hart & The Hurricanes, he was struck with how sweet and engaging she was. He couldn't wait to marry her. He found himself pushing away angry thoughts that he'd had to wait so long to find her; it served neither of them any good.

Staring into her gorgeous blue eyes, he let her dress fall to the floor and pool around her feet, leaving her before him in a pretty little lacy bra and panties. "You are perfect," he whispered.

She scoffed. "Hardly. But I'm happy you think so."

He kissed her lips, then slid his hand behind her and released the clasp on her bra. Sliding that off her body, he enjoyed the feel of her breasts in his hands, while she unbuttoned his shirt.

She pulled his shirt off his shoulders and let it fall to the floor. Stepping closer, she brushed her breasts against his chest and he moaned. "You feel perfect."

She chuckled. "So do you."

She unbuttoned his slacks and pushed them over his hips as he tugged her panties over hers.

They stepped away from their clothing, and he moved them three steps back until his legs hit the sectional in his Florida room. He sat down, pulling her onto his lap. The smile she graced him with was stunning, the moonlight shining across her glistening skin was incredible.

She lifted slightly, positioning his hard cock at her entrance, and slid down slowly. She moaned, "Damn you feel good inside of me."

He shook his head. "I have no words for how it feels to slide inside of you. It's what I imagine heaven must be like. Snug, warm, wet, and secure. All the good things."

She began moving up and down on him, her breasts swaying as she moved. His hands enjoyed their fullness.

Their eyes locked together as she brought them to pleasure, slowly at first, then faster as they both neared their happy ending. He loved their sultry nights out here in this room. The heat mixed with their burning passion was everything he'd ever wanted. Life was so good he thought as Hanna cried out, "Quinn." He grinned and followed her over the edge of pleasure. "Hanna."

Are you excited to find out who is going to catch Jace Marriott? Find out in Seductive Nights!

If reading paperback - go to this link - https://www.pjfiala.com/books/seductive-nights/

I'd love to keep in touch with you and share about new releases, sales, recipes, and other fun things with you. If this sounds like something you'd enjoy, join my newsletter by clicking this link - https://www.subscribepage.com/PJsReadersClub

ALSO BY PJ FIALA

I'm fortunate to be able to do what I love. It's a blessing.

My list of written works has gotten so long I needed to move it to my website! How's that for blessed?

Anyway, click the link below to see the list of all of my books.

Thank you so much for reading.

Click here to see a list of all of my books with descriptions

If you're reading a paperback, go to -

https://www.pjfiala.com/bibliography-pj-fiala/

MEET PJ

Writing has been a desire my whole life. Once I found the courage to write, life changed for me in the most profound way. Bringing stories to readers that I'd enjoy reading and creating characters that are flawed, but lovable is such a joy.

When not writing, I'm with my family doing something fun. My husband, Gene, and I are bikers and enjoy riding to new locations, meeting new people and generally enjoying this fabulous country we live in.

I come from a family of veterans. My grandfather, father, brother, two sons, and one daughter-in-law are all veterans. Needless to say, I am proud to be an American and proud of the service my amazing family has given.

My online home is https://www.pjfiala.com.
You can connect with me on
Facebook: https://www.facebook.com/PJFialaAuthor
Instagram: https://www.Instagram.com/PJFiala.
YouTube: https://youtube.com/@PJFiala
TikTok: https://www.tiktok.com/@pjfiala?lang=en
If you prefer to email, go ahead, I'll respond - pjfiala@ pjfiala.com.

COPYRIGHT

I. Title – SULTRY NIGHTS
ISBN-13: 978-1-959386-56-8